The Painted Ladies

A Sidra Smart Mystery
Book Five

Sylvia Dickey Smith

2020 White Bird Publications, LLC 3rd Edition

Copyright © 2018 by Sylvia Dickey Smith

Published in the United States
by White Bird Publication, LLC, Texas
http://www.whitebirdpublications.com

Paperback ISBN 978-1-63363-445-9
eBook ISBN 978-1-63363-446-6
Library of Congress Control Number 2019954640

PRINTED IN THE UNITED STATES OF AMERICA

To my children,
Jim, Jon Mark, Anissa,
Russell, and Robin

Author's Note:

I often wonder if houses have souls. Do they celebrate happy times with their owners and hurt when their owners hurt? Do wounds inflicted within their walls soak into the very structure; permeable surfaces, open orifices, bullet-riddled wood, cracks in the wall, spilled blood, or left behind energy of the departed?

If so, how do these houses manifest it? Is that what I feel when I walk into a house and know something's not quite right?

If it isn't that, then what is it?

Other books
by Sylvia

Original Cyn

Sacred Lessons from Wilderness Wandering

A War of Her Own

Sidra Smart Mystery Series

Dance on His Grave
Deadly Sins, Deadly Secrets
Dead Wreckoning
The Swamp Whisperer

The Painted Ladies

White Bird
Publications

I believe there is much more
going on here
on this Planet
and in our Universe
than what we see,
what we hear,
or what we know.

PROLOGUE
If These Walls Could Talk

The moon refused to shine that night. So did the stars.

However, the kerosene-fed flames lit the black sky like hell erupted through the earth's mantle, eager for its next victim.

Even while I watched the inferno consume my mother's remains, I knew her to be the lucky one. My sisters, Lilly and Scarlet took it harder than I did, but that's because they didn't know the whole story. In time they learned, though, and now stay joined at the hip—see one, see the other—deceiving them selves into believing safety comes in numbers.

I know the truth. No place is safe. The negative vortex simply left the flaming building and moved next door. Over the years, that negative vortex attracted the desperate, the needy, and the vulnerable, all who sold themselves to survive.

Despite all who try to live or work in these buildings, no one stays for long. We know because the past binds us here, forces us to keep vigil. So we suffer every day—day after day—night after night—decade after decade, for over a century now.

Noises, odors, the influence of thoughts, feelings, addictions, patterns, and even physical feelings negatively impact those who try to live within our walls. It grows worse at night when the energies wander the rooms as though lost in their search for revenge, seeking justice, seeking peace, forgiveness even.

And we live through it—day after day, year after year, over and over and over again.

Folks know me as Fancy, the yellow one.

Lilly is blue. Scarlet—well—she's Pepto pink.

Local folks call us The Painted Ladies, tall, slender women of courage—survivors.

If they only knew that we cling to the hillside of sanity, our fingertips loosening in the crumbling dirt.

Miss Fancy

Chapter One

Pave the planet. Get it over with, the bumper sticker warned. Anyone familiar with downtown Houston, Texas knew the city fulfilled its part of that global assignment. Only the needs of a grief-stricken young woman named Belle Anderson had the power to drag Sidra back to *concrete chaos.*

Belle, twenty-four was the only child of Reverend Avery Anderson and his wife Lillian. Her world-famous father pastored a mega-mega-church in downtown Houston—until his private plane crashed into a Colorado mountainside. The mega church lost its beloved leader and Belle lost both her parents.

Sidra mailed a card and flowers, but didn't attend the funeral. She wondered if her ex-husband Sam had gone to the services. He always acted as if he and Avery were best buddies. Then again, Avery made everyone feel like his best friend. Charisma oozed from the man. Avery and Lillian ran in different social circles. Theirs consisted of the rich and famous. Sam and Sidra's circles had not.

The Andersons gave the impression of a happy couple, but something about their relationship puzzled Sidra. Lillian was as quiet as Avery was outgoing. Not unusual in itself, but something lurked behind her eyes that unsettled Sidra. Tragic as the plane crash and fiery deaths had been, the news soon dropped off the front page. Sidra hadn't thought about it for weeks until yesterday when the couple's daughter Belle called The Third Eye. She requested an appointment with Sidra, but in Houston, instead of Sidra's office in Orange, Texas. Seems Belle's family attorney set up an unexpected appointment with Belle for tomorrow, now today, but would not reveal the reason for the meeting. Since the estate had been settled, this secretive meeting caused Belle alarm. She felt a need for support, but not from anyone she knew in Houston. For some odd reason, she called Sidra to accompany her.

Sidra followed the GPS through town and beyond, until she reached an upscale neighborhood. Very upscale.

Rumors of the Anderson's twelve-million-dollar mansion filled the newspapers and television, but her mouth dropped when the GPS voice reported she'd reached her destination. She gawked at massive black gates sporting an embossed AA logo. A security camera whirred, and the gate opened. A long, palm-tree-lined drive led to the Avery mansion—or palace—she wasn't sure.

Sidra stepped out of her car as Belle opened the massive front doors and skipped down the drive towards her. Something about the girl's long glossy black hair and matching ensemble reminded Sidra of a raven. She'd read that ravens were intelligent birds—relied on logic to guide their actions. Perhaps that said something about Belle, too.

Sam had always remarked how unlucky Belle was

that she didn't get her mother's picture-perfect looks. Sidra disagreed. Something in the girl's aura radiated warmth, sincerity, and an authenticity missing in her parents.

"You came," Belle called out, surprise coating her voice.

"Of course I came." Sidra hoped her smile covered a chest full of discomfort and hesitation. She wasn't accustomed to visiting mansions; however, it wasn't the elegance of the place that intimidated Sidra. It was not having a clue what to say to someone who, in an instant, lost both parents. Sam, always the minister, taught her to remind them of God's promise to never give us any more than we could bear.

Bull shit.

Sidra wrapped her arms around the thin shoulders of the young woman. "You doing okay, Sweetheart?"

"Better with you here. It's nice to be with someone other than one of Father's groupies. They are all so caught up in their own grief they pass it on to me."

Sidra didn't know what to say. Instead, she squeezed a little tighter.

"I'll drive," Belle said. "I know where we're going. Your car is fine parked there."

The two got in the Infrared Lexus RC F 350 and headed out the gates.

Sidra tried not to gawk at the automobile's elaborate interior, but couldn't help but brush her hand across the rich black leather seat.

"Thank you for going with me, today."

"Happy to, but I must admit your call surprised me."

"I'm sure it did, since we hardly know each other. I've heard of you, though, and admired your bravery when you left Reverend Smart and struck out on your own. I often wished my mother…" She waved off the end of the sentence.

Belle turned the conversation to surprises in wills,

admitting how shocked she was when she learned the magnitude of the fortune her parents—her father—had accumulated. "No one can say religion doesn't pay well," she scoffed.

"Folks say my father died a happy man, but his happiness didn't work for me. At times, I almost wish I felt guilty but… Never mind. I didn't mean to go there. It just slipped out."

They rode in silence for a couple of miles. Sidra waited.

"I don't know what I'm walking into at this meeting," Belle said, finding her voice again. "I've got this heavy knot in the pit of my stomach telling me I don't want to hear it." She glanced from the highway to Sidra and back. "I've read about you in the papers—how you inherited your brother's private detective business in Orange."

Sidra laughed. "Can you imagine how much I knew, or a better term might be didn't know, about the detective business?"

"I love the name, *The Third Eye: Intuitive Investigations*."

"Well, wait until you see the humongous blue eye on the sign out front. It's hideous, but my brother loved it— and it seems to fit. He was rather psychic, and—"

"You are too."

"Excuse me?" A multi-colored bomb exploded in Sidra's head.

Belle kept her eyes on the freeway, but a smile crept around her mouth. "Don't tell me you didn't know?"

"I… I…"

"What? Haven't admitted it to yourself?"

"I guess I haven't but…"

"But you know it. What? Clairaudient?"

Sidra's jaw dropped. "What makes you think so?"

"I sense it. I am, too. That is what bothered the hell out of my father. Or I should say scared the shit out of him."

Sidra chuckled. "I guess it would. Mind telling me more?"

"Happy to, but it will have to wait. We're here." Belle pulled into a garage, parked then checked hair and makeup. She sucked through her teeth and shoved the mirror closed. "I can't even look in a mirror without my father's niggling displeasure staring back at me. He never approved of anything I did. The way I dressed made me look too *easy*, he argued. Reflected badly on him, and he had *an image to maintain*. Miniskirts, spike heels and an all-red wardrobe led him to see me as a rebel. Maybe if he'd liked them a little, or at least hadn't nagged me about them, I wouldn't have been so obstinate, but..." She grabbed her shoulder bag and the two exited the car.

"The elevator doors open directly into the law office of Maxxwell Parker," Belle explained. "Maxx served not only as my father's legal counsel, but also for my father's church—in other words, a tax-free corporate lawyer."

Sidra sensed Belle didn't care much for Maxx.

"Probably because he wears his dark hair combed back in a pompadour like my father," Belle said, reading Sidra's thoughts.

The receptionist explained Mr. Parker was on a phone call and invited them to sit while they waited—shouldn't be long, she said. Sidra followed Belle, who chose a plush chair near glass windows overlooking the downtown skyline.

Seldom is one prepared to lose both parents in one fell swoop. Yet it happened, and Belle still breathed. Sidra understood the feeling. The untimely death of her brother and the subsequent inheritance of The Third Eye still took her breath away.

Her thoughts skipped to the last thing Belle said before they got out of the car. Psychic? Really? She'd never thought of herself as anything other than normal— whatever normal was. Warren believed her to be psychic, like him, and as a result left her a detective agency that specialized in intuitive investigations.

Belle looked confused, clueless, like the city she knew so well wasn't the same. It felt like the whole town grieved with her—and indeed it did. Her father was, or had been, one of the most popular men in the city and with the help of the Internet, the media, and a multitude of best-selling books, perhaps the country. He traveled the world with his message of happiness and abundance.

"You know," Belle said, her words soft, contemplative, "my father died a happy man, at least I suppose he did."

"Miss Anderson? Mr. Parker will see you now. Follow the hallway to your right and take the first door on the left."

The two walked to Parker's private office. Belle gave a soft rap and they walked inside.

He stood behind a massive, ornate desk. Nothing lay on it but a single packet of papers.

"Good morning, Belle. Good to see you. How are you holding up, sweetheart?"

His quiet words sounded kind enough, an attempt at warmth, but something about the man didn't sound authentic to Sidra. She got the feeling he acted a role—or roles, as the case may be.

"Hanging on by a thread, if you want the truth. Trying to figure out who I am, or who I want to be, now that I'm not in the spotlight of the world-famous Reverend Avery Anderson."

"I can imagine."

"By the way, this is my friend, Sidra Smart. I invited her to come with me this morning."

"I see. Welcome, Ms. Smart. Please have a seat, both of you." He indicated the chairs in front of his desk.

"As you know," Belle continued, "I never liked the spotlight. I hated it. However, now that I'm no one, I'm not quite sure who I am."

"Well, one thing for certain, you won't have to worry

about supporting yourself. Of course they didn't realize you'd inherit it this early, but…"

He cleared his throat and picked up the packet of papers. "As you know, we read the will when we met with the judge…" He glanced at Sidra, as though unsure whether to continue in her presence, then shrugged and went on. "There's one piece of property we haven't addressed yet. Judge Neighbors and I thought it would be easier if you and I talked about it in private—off the record."

His face flushed. Embarrassment? Or guilt?

"Good lord, more property is exactly what I need. Where?" Belle pulled her jacket tighter.

"This is the title to the property. When you read it, you'll see the deed involves a large piece of land with three houses in Hot Springs, Arkansas."

"You're kidding—surely." She chortled, expecting him to see the humor.

He didn't.

"Wait a minute, you're telling me… Why on earth would my mom and dad own even one house, let alone three, in another city—in another state? I don't remember us ever going there or them talking about it."

He glanced at the paper, tapped it with an index finger. "Actually, your father didn't own them. Your mother did."

"My mother?" Belle's jaw dropped lower. She gawked from Sidra to Maxx to the papers in his hands. "I don't know a single soul in Arkansas. As far as I know, neither did my mother. Never been there, never *wanted* to go there."

"Evidently Rev. and Mrs. Anderson never went there either," he said, "at least your father didn't. Your mother went a time or two to check on the property. My understanding is she had a property manager in charge. They provided upkeep and lease oversight."

He swallowed hard then tugged on the collar of his

dress shirt. "I'm not surprised you didn't know about this property. As a matter of fact, your father never wanted you to know anything about it—shunned it even. Left it to me to look after."

"How did they, or how did my mother happen to own them? Did she buy the property sight unseen or what?"

Maxx Parker averted his eyes. "Ah, let's see if this says." He pulled a pen out of his pocket and used it as he scanned the page.

If stonewalling had an odor, rotten fish would escape notice.

Chapter Two

Maxx's response left Sidra suspect. He knew more than he admitted. Much more.

"Don't feed me bullshit, Maxx," Belle said with a blast of energy. "You know the answer to that question. Otherwise the whole topic would have surfaced at Probate Court."

The pen slipped out of his fingers and hit the floor. He made a production of collecting it, then unbuttoning his shirt collar and loosening his tie, all without a glance their way. "Just let me…double check…my facts," he said. "Oh, okay, here's what I was looking for."

Belle looked ready to explode. "You've stalled long enough Maxx Parker. I don't care what the papers say. I want to know how my parents—or at least my mother— came to own these houses? Answer my damn question."

He flushed, sucked in a deep breath. "Seems like," he flipped a couple of pages, "your mother, yeah, she inherited them."

"Okay, then why didn't she sell them?"

"It's a long story, Belle. I shouldn't be the one to tell you—your parents should have—years ago. Either told you or done something with these structures. Your father wanted to, but since they were in your mother's name and a part of her inheritance, he had no power to do so." Maxx chuckled. "Only time I ever knew your mother to go against him."

Belle smiled. "My mom could take a stand; she just didn't often take one against my dad. Saved those for me." Tears formed and rolled down her cheeks. "Give me a minute." She fumbled for a tissue.

Composure regained, she continued. "She could infuriate me, maybe as much as I infuriated her. But we didn't fight like my dad and I did."

Sidra knew what it was like for a preacher's kid to be accused of not being a good role model. Sam always bitched at their daughter. How he needed her to set the example for the youth group, and how her doing the opposite threatened his job. Avery Anderson certainly didn't have to worry about the slightest possibility of that happening. On every television station in the country at one time or another, preaching about how God wanted to bless people with riches—abundance to all who served God like he did. The preacher got rich because folks thought if they followed what he told them to do, they'd be rich too, so the money poured in—private jets, fancy homes, country clubs, invited guest on TV shows.

However, none of that had anything to do with Belle anymore. It was all in the past. Her parents were gone— and she the sole heir of all the wealth her father accumulated from others. Decisions once his, were now Belle's. Wow. What an earthquake for a young woman.

"So what have you done with the property all this

time," Belle asked, bringing Sidra's thoughts back to the present.

"Paid the taxes on it and kept it in some semblance of repair, maintained the contract with the property manager."

"So the houses have not been vacant all these years?"

"No, not really. From time to time, the management company rented them out to local businesses. I think there's been a couple of hair salons, a massage parlor, that sort of thing, but for some reason or the other, renters never stay very long."

That sounded vague, suspicious even, like something—or someone drove them away.

"Are they rented now, or are they vacant?"

Maxxwell cleared his throat. "Hmm, well, I guess you could say vacant."

"Are they vacant or not?"

"Vacant, yes. Have been for several years. Every now and then someone rents them for a short period of time, vacation rentals, that sort of thing."

"I assume they're furnished?"

"In a manner of speaking, yes."

Could the man be more vague? Something motivated him, but what?

Belle stared at the floor. "Arkansas, you say. What town? They are in a town aren't they?"

He picked up the Warranty Deed as if unsure, himself. "Let's see, yes, Hot Springs, a nice town, really. Tourists, horse races, bathhouses, lots to see.

Sidra had heard of Hot Springs with its hot mineral baths, art galleries, magician, and music festivals—even haunted ghost tours.

"So how did you say my mother acquired this property?"

"Like I said, handed down through a couple of generations."

Something about Maxxwell Parker's response lacked…something. He knew more than he revealed.

Evidently Belle felt it too.

"It's been a long time… Let me take another look. I know it was some kind of inheritance." He turned behind him and fetched a file folder, then fingered through a stack of paperwork inside. "Seems your mother inherited the property shortly before she married your father. I always felt like the inheritance embarrassed your mother and humiliated your father. Not real sure why. They never would talk about it much. Seemed to be a sore subject between them."

"Strange—but then again, not all that unusual for my parents. Most things…well, you know…"

Maxxwell Parker cleared his throat again. "I expect there will be compensation from the airplane manufacturer. Seems the malfunction led to the crash, then again, there's no way to know until the authorities finish the investigation. In the meantime, your father invested wisely. He left enough you won't ever have to worry about money."

"Can you get the realtor in Hot Springs to list these houses? The last thing I need right now is a trip. Just sell them and be done with it."

"We could, sure, and this is none of my business, but these houses have been in your mother's family for more than a century. Something tells me it might be worth your while to get to know more about your mother and her family. She never said, but I got the idea they held a special importance to her. It might be in your best interest to get acquainted with her a little better. Those houses should do it."

"I never knew my mom to have any other family except us. She always called herself an only child, orphaned at a young age. Grew up in foster homes, mostly."

"I'm not certain your mother gave you the whole story, sweetheart." Parker's voice softened, revealing something Sidra couldn't quite touch—but he knew more than he admitted. "Why don't you go check them out? Then, if you want to list them, I can handle it for you. I have a feeling that if you dig, you'll learn a lot about your mother. She might even have relatives living there—or folks who knew her family."

He smoothed his pompadour, as if he feared a hair might be out of place—or *he* was.

"Since you have no other family left, it might be good to take a trip. Besides, Hot Springs is a neat little town. I went there a couple of times to check on the property for your parents."

He paused, tapped his forehead, and then almost as an afterthought, said, "Jefferson—Jefferson, Texas—there is something about that east Texas town. It figures into all of this somehow, but I'm not sure how."

His off-the-cuff comment made Sidra shiver, but Belle appeared to have missed it. Instead, she chewed her bottom lip, like her thoughts were elsewhere.

"I have leave time built up at the newspaper," she said, almost to herself. "Maybe they could do without me for a few days. Or better yet—maybe I could write a travel article. Folks are always looking for places to take vacations."

"Sweetheart," Maxx said. "I've known you and your family a long time. I suppose your father told me things he never told anyone else—couldn't, and keep the persona he'd worked hard to perfect. Lawyers become sort of therapists to clients like him. I know the two of you struggled, and I know why."

Belle straightened, threw back her shoulders, and looked Maxxwell Parker straight in the eye. "What are you saying? What do I not know that you do? Tell me."

Her words sounded like an order. She hesitated, as if she might take them back. She didn't.

"I don't mean to be mysterious or secretive—but you know, when people keep relating to you like you are a therapist, in time, you learn stuff." He gave a nervous laugh, like he'd stepped into a sticky topic. "When the time is right, I think I can help you understand your father and mother a little better—and why you struggled with them. But now isn't the time. First you need to learn more about your mother—and her mother, and maybe even her mother's mother."

"My great grandmother?" She gestured with her palms up and open. "You mean to tell me these houses go back to…to…my mom's mom's mom? That's weird. I never met her, but anytime I'd ask about her family, even if Mom tried to tell me, Dad shushed her. I can still see the pain in Mom's face when he did. I knew…well, actually, I didn't know—not a thing—other than Dad wouldn't let Mother talk about her mother or grandmother. That isn't—wasn't right." Belle jumped to her feet and paced the room.

"I knew your mom…" He choked and cleared his throat. "…and your mom's mom—even your great grandmother in a way. You didn't ask my opinion, but I'll give it. Go see the property. Connect with your mother's past. Here's the ugly truth. Your mother lost herself when she married your dad for whatever reasons—which were valid to her at the time. Guess they stayed valid—until after you became a young woman, and she saw you—the person you grew into, and recognized herself and your grandmother. The rebellion, the—shall we say…er…your determination. Your strength, your strong will. Your love of life, your passion."

His words evidently captured Belle's attention. Looking spellbound, she returned to her chair, hands in her lap and eyes glued on Maxx.

"Your mother shoved her identity deep and covered it with the persona required of her. I went to your dad's church. I saw her day after day—the mask. She hid behind it so long it became no longer removable. Go learn about her and your grandmothers, who they were on the inside—before… Well, you know."

In one instant, Sidra sat listening, her mind absorbing every nuance of energy between the other two, curious about the story behind this ever more perplexing family dynamic. Trying to fit the pieces into a puzzle more complex than one might imagine.

The flash of a raging orange fireball instantly filled the room threatening to suck all of them inside its core. The room spun, carrying Sidra deeper into the flaming vortex. She heard herself scream—was it her, or someone else? Her fingers gripped the chair arms, too fearful to let go.

Then it disappeared as fast as it came, leaving behind the strongest odor of—cigar smoke? Maxx and Belle still chatted. Apparently, they saw nothing, and heard nor smelled anything.

Goosies popped out on Sidra's arm. Her grandmother used to say someone walked over your grave when that happened. Since Sidra wasn't dead, she wasn't sure, but the conversation between Belle and Maxx stirred something from the other side. Was she the only one who felt it?

She looked at the other two, still engaged in heavy conversation, seemingly oblivious to…whatever…

"You've got the money," Maxx was saying, "take the trip, whether or not the paper gives you an assignment for a travel article or not. Go. Find your mother, your grandmother, and your great grandmother there—for when you do, you will find Belle Anderson."

"At least it would get me away from all these well-meaning church members. They're nice, but—"

"They're driving you crazy."

"Exactly." She pounded her knee. "I can just hear what my father would say about all this."

By now, Maxxwell had moved from behind his desk. A flash of sunlight through the window appeared like a silver halo over his head. "Sweetheart, go. Just trust me. Go. When you find your answers, come back and we'll talk about your mom and dad."

It hit Sidra, that when they entered Maxx's office, he seemed standoffish, almost like he wanted to duck the meeting.

However, by now he came across almost—what? Cuddly? She tucked the information away but made a mental note to keep her eyes open.

Belle must have noticed too, for her demeanor did a one-eighty. It went from grief-stricken and shocked, to panicked. Sidra took her by the elbow and led her out of his office and to the firm's private elevator.

When the doors closed, Belle put her hand on her forehead and said, "I've heard of a person's head spinning—but never like this. I thought I knew everything there was to know about my parents." A sarcastic laugh slipped out. "Does a person ever really know another person? Especially when the other person feels responsible to set the perfect example for…" The elevator doors opened, a couple stepped out of the elevator, and walked into the law office. "…the whole damn world?"

Chapter Three

Belle rolled her eyes and gave Sidra a who-gives-a-rat's-ass look as the elevator doors closed behind the couple.

"Do you know those folks?" Sidra attempted to suppress a chuckle. It didn't work.

"Nah, but they probably recognized me. Most likely they're members of my father's congregation, along with most everyone else in the greater Houston area."

Both women grew quiet. Sidra had no idea what occupied Belle's thoughts, but only one topic occupied hers, the fireball and the cigar smoke. She considered asking Belle about them, but changed her mind. Instead, she tucked the sensory matter away. Perhaps Warren saw and might mention it—thing is, she never knew when he'd show up.

The elevator stopped and the doors opened to the

parking garage. Soon as they stepped out, Sidra's stomach growled.

"Sounds like you're hungry." Belle laughed. "There's a coffee shop next door. Want to grab a sandwich?"

"I think we better, or we'll have to listen to my belly complain all the way back to your house."

They took a left as they walked out of the garage, and into an upscale café. A group of young professionals sat hunched around a corner table laughing, talking and sipping America's favorite, most expensive, hot beverage. Behind them, posters plastered the walls. Each poster advertised luscious-looking cups of coffee decorated with heart-shaped cream. Alongside the posters, huge burlap-looking bags of coffees from around the world invited customers to browse and buy.

They placed their order for sandwiches and coffee and found a table away from the noise.

Sidra waited for Belle to speak first, but after a long awkward pause, Sidra decided to jump in and address what certainly must be where Belle's thoughts had taken her.

"I don't want to sound like I'm prying, that is not my intent, but would you like to talk about your parents, your mother or dad? Maxx? You've just received a big shock. Maybe processing it might help."

Belle didn't respond. Just kept staring at her hands clenched on the table, inhaling long deep breaths and then releasing them slow and easy.

Sidra wondered if Belle heard what she said but waited in silence.

When Belle found her voice, it came so soft and low Sidra strained to hear.

"My dad and I were always very close until…"

Silence.

"…Until I hit puberty."

More silence.

The server came with their food and drinks.

After the server left, Belle continued in the same soft voice. "I have neat memories of us when I was a child—I knew he loved me. But it all changed at puberty. I never understood why. I felt his discomfort around me, especially if we were close together."

Belle grew quiet. Sidra wondered where her thoughts had taken her.

"Then, he went on a campaign to *save my soul* and as long as he lived, he never stopped."

"How did you handle that?" Sidra took a bite out of her sandwich and returned the rest of it to her plate.

"Humph." Belle gave a derisive laugh. "I'll tell you how I handled it; I never stopped claiming my soul for myself."

Silence. Sidra waited.

"He never accepted me for who I was, always tried to make me over into who he thought I should be. The perfect shining example of what he believed to be true—mostly—but also what would not embarrass him to his adoring public. His church is one of the biggest mega churches in Houston, if not the biggest. Those people had him on such a high pedestal of perfection I could never keep up nor match—or want to match it. Adoration and accolades as being the holiest of holy never fit me—and nothing less fit him."

"With Mom in the middle." Sidra spoke softly. She understood being in the middle. She'd filled that spot between Sam and their two kids.

"Yet I adored him." Tears rolled down her cheeks and dripped on the tabletop.

Sidra rested her hands atop Belle's, now on top of the small table, and waited quietly.

"Don't get me wrong, I loved my mom, too, but... You know how I felt around her? Like this translucent glass shell surrounded her—keeping me, and everyone else away. She tried to be there for me, but I always felt something stood between us—and that got worse as I grew older."

"Puberty thing again?" Sidra asked.

"I guess. I don't know." Belle stared, unfocused, like time had turned in on itself and transported her to an earlier period and place.

She shook her head. "They both seemed like…like they were scared of me afterwards."

"Or scared for you, maybe?"

"Maybe." She sipped her coffee and nibbled on the corner of her sandwich.

Sidra had already inhaled her food.

A couple came in, ordered take-out and left. The crowd in the front corner had added a couple more chairs and people to their group.

"So what do you think about me going to Hot Springs, and checking out these homes my mother inherited? The whole thing seems so absurd. What do I care if she owned property there? Sell them and add the dollars to the already overflowing coffers they left behind."

"My experience, sweetheart, is the best way around an issue is through it. So yes, I think you should go check them out and in the process learn more about your mother and her family."

"Would you go with me?" She looked Sidra in the eye. "On retainer, of course. I'm really not sure what I'm going to find, and I need someone to help me make sense out of it."

"Whoa, give me a couple minutes to wrap my head around all this." Sidra glanced away, deep in thought when a high-pitched, grating voice cried "Hi, Belle."

Sidra looked up to see a young redheaded female shooting I-feel-so-sorry-for-you-but-I'm-so-glad-it's-not-me arrows at Belle. "We are devastated about our loss of Pastor and our beautiful Lillian. You holding up okay? We've been missing you at church."

"Oh, hi Dee Ann," Belle murmured. "Yeah, I… I—"

"Now's the time when we must depend on God's

promise. He said he'd never send us more than we can bear."

"Yeah, right, you go right on doing that." Belle stood and gathered her trash. "You about ready to go, Sidra?"

Sidra took a final swig of coffee and trailed Belle to the door. Behind her, the Dee Ann woman said, "Well! I never! How rude!"

"It's people like that who drive me crazy," Belle said, with a snort. "They mean well, but they irritate the hell out of me. She's thankful all right—thankful the loss is mine, not hers."

All the way to the car Sidra's head swam with questions. Could she do this? Should she do this? Might her own past skew her ability to be unbiased—to see events clearly? What about Annie? Slider? Ben?

Belle burned rubber as she sped through the parking garage and out into heavy Houston traffic. She weaved in and out at a speed apparently matching her anxiety.

Sidra held on for good measure. What would an out of town trip be like with this young woman, obviously more comfortable with speed than safety?

"You sure you wouldn't rather take a friend with you? A full-time retainer could get expensive."

Not to mention the risk of life and limb.

Belle sputtered. "You must be kidding. I have more money than I know what to do with. I might as well get busy spending it. Besides, I'm a journalist for the Houston paper. Maybe I can write a travel article on Hot Springs. Maxx said the city attracted a lot of tourists. That should work, don't you think?"

"I… I don't know… I suppose so." Sidra held her foot ready to slam on the non-existent brakes on the passenger side as space between their vehicle and the one in front of them loomed at an uncomfortable distance.

Belle must have noticed, for she eased off the gas and moved back into the flow of traffic. "I really hope you will. You've listened to me more than my parents ever did."

Wow. Could she say no to this young woman, obviously in need of answers?

Sidra's thoughts went to Aunt Annie and wondered if she dare leave her aunt at the office by herself for several days—wondered if The Third Eye would survive it—or the town. Then she had Slider to contend with. Maybe Ben would…

"When were you thinking of going? I'll need to clear my calendar and get someone to take care of my dog Slider, that sort of thing."

"Bring your dog, I'm okay with that. I'll have Jenkins with me. The two can be buddies."

"I might have to. My aunt and I live together. I'd say she could take care of him, but she has this humongous tabby cat that rules the roost. If I'm not there, Slider gets the short end of the stick—locked outside and stuff. I might talk with my fiancé and see if Slider can stay with him.

"Okay, how about meeting me at my house tomorrow morning early? Think you can be ready that soon? One of my dad's many vehicles is a Lincoln Navigator. We'll take it and have plenty of room to stretch out."

Two dogs cooped up in the car—even though it was a Navigator—for hours. Yes, she'd talk to Ben.

"In the meantime, I've got to talk to my boss at the newspaper. Maybe she won't have a problem with me taking the time, especially if I send her articles about Arkansas."

Belle startled Sidra when she made a quick lane change, pulled off I-10 and into the parking lot designated for one of the larger Houston newspapers.

"Well," Belle turned off the ignition. "Since you've been on retainer since you left home this morning, let's keep it going. From now until we get the issue with these houses settled, the bills are on me, plus your commission."

Sidra wasn't sure her response, but she thought she nodded.

"Perfect. I can afford whatever price you bill me, so don't worry about that. Right now, I got to do this while my curiosity is in charge. Otherwise, I might never have the ovaries to do it."

"Why did you stop here?" Sidra looked at the buildings alongside the street.

"This is the newspaper building where I work. I'm hoping you will go with me to talk to my boss. If I go up there on my own with this far-fetched story, she'll call the loony patrol. She's already worried about me. With you, she won't worry so much."

Sidra's mind reeled as they entered the elevator and it sped to the top floor. It opened on a maze of desks and cubicles and hallways. She followed Belle through a row of doors along the wall, clueless to how she got there and where it would end.

Belle rapped on one of the opaque glass doors and pushed it open. "Afternoon, Beckette, can we come in and talk?"

"We?"

The two entered the large, corporate office overlooking the city skyline.

"This is Sidra Smart, a private detective."

Beckette's expression went from confused to concerned. "Nice to meet you, ma'am. Is everything okay, Belle?"

In the seconds hanging between the question and the answer, Sidra wondered how Belle would explain their upcoming trip, about the houses, and the family secrets.

Belle didn't. Instead, she requested time off and an assignment to write a travel article.

"A travel article? Of where?" Beckette looked puzzled.

"Hot Springs, Arkansas."

"Are you sure this is the time for you to—right after—well, you know, all you've been through?" She walked around her desk and put her arm around Belle's shoulders. "Honey, I don't have a problem with you taking time off—extended time off—to go do what you need to do, go wherever you need to go, but why Hot Springs, Arkansas? Maybe somewhere like—Hawaii, the Caribbean, or Europe? Where you can really get away."

Belle didn't respond. Instead, she backed up to a chair and collapsed.

Genuine concern clouded Beckette's face. She looked to be middle-aged—closer to Belle's mother's age. Perhaps a mother-daughter bond had developed between them. Sidra hoped so.

Belle fought tears that ignored her effort. The floodgates opened and once began, didn't stop for several minutes. Sidra and Beckette both pulled chairs near Belle and sat quietly while the dam broke.

Sidra gave Beckette a questioning look, wondering whether Belle had cried since the accident. Beckette shook her head.

"No wonder." Sid spoke softly, not wanting to interrupt Belle's long overdue cry.

After much sniffling and nose blowing, the tears slowed and, and the floodgate of water turned into an avalanche of words.

"I had the television on," Belle dabbed her eyes with a tissue, "when the reporter broke in and said a private plane crashed in a heavily wooded area outside Colorado City. I knew the plane had been my dad's, and neither he nor my mother survived. Felt it in my bones. Why or how I knew, I have no idea. I just knew. It hit home even stronger when the news reporter indicated that the deceased couple were a well-known minister and his wife. No one was better known than my dad. He took great pride in the fact of his mega-church—*his* mega-church—was the envy of so many other ministers. He didn't gloat. He simply had a way of *acting* so humble about the whole thing—blaming his success on God. I'm not positive God had a thing to do with any of it.

"I don't have the same relationship with my dad's God. Or the God of so many hundreds of people that filled his pews, that gave the money—that allowed us to live in a castle, drive luxury vehicles, and wear the finest clothes. Bugged the hell out of me if you want to know the truth."

Beckette collected a paper cup, filled it water from the blue dispenser, and handed it to Belle. She gulped it, crushed the paper cup, and slung it across the room.

"Dad's magnetism overpowered me, my mom, everyone within his reach. It took every ounce of strength I possessed to convince him to let me live in the guest cottage out behind the main house. I figured if I could, in time, I'd move out from under his control and into my own apartment. I've lived in the cottage since college, but I still hadn't been able to force the next step—not when my mother gave me that pitiful look that said if I left, I abandoned her. The more Dad focused on me, the less he tried to control Mom. I knew. Mom did too. I often wondered if Daddy realized it. Now, I'll never know."

She looked up from the wadded tissues in her hands. "You two don't need to hear all this baggage."

"We're okay, at least I'm okay." Beckette lifted an eyebrow and glanced at Sidra.

"Keep going, sweetheart. I'm on the clock now. Remember?"

The three chuckled.

"It took years for me to recognize my role in the family—to take the heat off my mom. As long as I rebelled, my mother could stand behind her man and look all meek and mild and submissive."

Oh, boy, Sidra thought, what about her daughter, Sam, and what it must have been like for her growing up. Had her rebellion been a result of the same pressures?

"What the hell do I do now since, in one fell swoop—or crash—both of my parents were yanked out of my life? Must I still rebel? Is there a need to go against…what?"

The room grew silent.

"When I heard the news, my first feeling was relief—freedom—like a life sentence had been commuted by an airplane malfunction…"

Belle sat quietly for a couple of minutes, then picked up where she left off. "Don't get me wrong. I loved my parents. Dearly. The pain eats at my insides. Hate and love all mixed up, churns, jerks me first one way, and then the other. It would be so much easier if I could claim one emotion and reject the other. But it doesn't seem to work that way—not for me, at least. Anyway, I'm done talking about this for now."

Beckette clasped Belle's hands and the two stood and embraced. "Take the time you need, sweetheart. I don't care where you go or what you do. If you want to write a travel article, do so. Please stay in touch. Send me a text or email."

Sidra and Belle headed to the ladies' room for repairs then returned to the car.

"You know, Belle, I'm thinking a good place to start the healing process may well be in understanding your mother—learning who she was and where she came from. Perhaps the answers lay in this secretive property in some small town in the middle of Arkansas."

"Maybe so. Go figure."

Half an hour later, they drove inside the black *pearly* gates and parked in front of the mansion.

"Don't worry about a thing, Belle," Sidra said as the two exited. "Pack your bag and have the Navigator gassed and ready. I'll make hotel reservations in Hot Springs. I guarantee we will get to the bottom of the history of these houses your mother and her family owned, or my name is not Sidra Smart."

Chapter Four

After Sidra left, Belle headed to the enormous chef's kitchen, trailed by Jenkins, her red longhaired spaniel.

"First, things first, huh Jenkins." She reached into the cabinet for one of her mother's priceless crystal stemware.

After the funeral a few weeks ago, she'd gone straight home, collected a couple bottles of wine from the chiller in the guesthouse out back—wine and chiller both hidden from her father. Now, she selected a bottle of Merlot, poured herself a glass, and settled into a chair near the fireplace. She'd always thought the mansion *over the top*, but she did love the luxury of a fireplace in the kitchen. It added a sense of home missing elsewhere in the house. She punched the remote and the gas logs ignited. Jenkins waited until she settled in, then jumped into her lap.

"I'm so lucky I have you, sweetheart, and guess what, we are not only the proud owners of more house and land than we could use in the first place, but we now own three old houses somewhere in the middle of Arkansas. Now, Maxx has convinced me to go check them out."

Jenkins cocked her head and gave Belle a quizzical expression, then gave a little yelp, ran to the backdoor, and waited, panting, tongue hanging out the side of her mouth.

"You silly mutt," she said, laughter filling her voice. "Not today, sweetheart. We've got to pack, make phone calls, and such. I don't know how long we'll be gone, so…"

Jenkins scratched at the door, eager, whining.

"Yeah, I know; I don't have to tell you GO twice. Okay, let's head upstairs and get out the suitcases."

She debated whether or not to call Sawyer and tell him she'd be gone for a while but decided against it. Their strained relationship could well do with time apart. Besides, she had her cell phone. He might call, but he certainly would not drop in. At the cemetery, she'd looked to see if he attended, certain he would be there, but if he had, she missed him. One would think a boyfriend who professed his undying love would be at her side, despite the thousands of people gathered around the mausoleum. Not that she cared whether or not he came. If it hadn't been for the feeble attempt to satisfy her dad, she never would have dated a man on the church staff. Regardless of how far the chain stretched from Sawyer to her dad.

No sooner had she made the decision not to call, than the phone rang and Sawyer Stewart showed on the caller ID. Belle stared at Jenkins. "Should I answer it?"

The phone rang a couple more times.

Jenkins stared at her and barked.

"Okay, okay." She rested the glass of wine on the brick hearth and punched the button. "Hello."

"You doing okay?" Sawyer asked. "I saw you at the

cemetery, but there were so many people around you all the time I couldn't get close. I've called you several times since then, even come by the mansion, but…"

She shivered and turned up the thermostat.

It isn't the first time he's caused that reaction, Belle, her clenched gut whispered.

"I'm fine."

"What do you mean, fine? I've tried the gate intercom several times, but no one ever answers. Aren't the servants there?"

"Um, I've been rather busy. I was about to send you a text and let you know I will be out of town for a few days. Got an assignment from my boss. To work on a project."

"Oh? By text? You mean you were leaving town without a phone call?"

"Well, I'm not now. Plus, there is such a thing as cell phones, Sawyer. I've got a lot of details to address, to take care of before I leave."

"Did you meet with your lawyer? How'd it go?"

"Fine. We still must go through probate and all."

"I imagine your father left everything to you since you're an only child."

"He? My mother is—was—a partner in the will as well."

"True. Slip of the tongue. Since your dad was—"

"I know what you meant—she didn't earn any of the money, and Dad was King Kong."

"Actually, what I meant was, sometimes wills can be full of surprises. None of those, eh?"

"Surprises? What kind? Why should there be surprises?"

"I don't know, it…" He stuttered. "I thought… Seems like wills always contain surprises."

Silence.

"Well, okay, then," he continued, "I hope you'll stay in touch? I'll let folks at the church know you'll be out of town until further notice. If you need anything, you'll call the church office, I guess."

"Sure—for sure." Like hell she would.

"When are you leaving? Can we spend time together before you go? Maybe we could—"

"I'm packing as we speak." *Okay, not really a lie, but close.* Jenkins and I are leaving later this week."

"You're taking the dog?"

"Sounds like you think I shouldn't."

"No, no…"

Fact of the matter was, Sawyer didn't like Jenkins, and the feeling was mutual.

"Seems like she might be a bother, having to stop on the side of the road… Where'd you say you were going?"

"Actually, I don't think I did, but it is Arkansas.

"I—I'm—I didn't mean to sound critical. I just meant… So what town in Arkansas? Little Rock? That's the capital, isn't it? Surely… Never mind. Just stay in touch. I'm a little concerned about you driving that far by yourself. Keep me posted."

"If anyone needs to find me, they can talk to Maxxwell Parker. He knows where I am."

"Aren't you taking your cell phone? I can call you, can't I… Or is this a write-off?"

"Sure. You can call." Didn't mean she'd answer.

Why in the world had she allowed her father to talk her into dating Sawyer in the first place? At least she hadn't slept with him, not because he hadn't tried.

She finished off the glass of wine, then collected the plastic container of dog food from the mudroom and located it near the garage door. That's when it hit her. She had no more need to hide her cards. She rescued the deck from the bottom of the dog food container and disposed of the plastic bag where she kept them.

She spent the evening writing notes for the house staff about her assignment out of state, and with instructions to call as needed. Notified her father's accountant by email—telling him not to panic when he saw credit card charges from other states.

She packed a couple of bags, telling herself she'd pick up anything else she needed on the way. The deck of cards—cards she had kept hidden from her parents—lay on top of her clothes. She zipped the suitcases and loaded them, the dog kennel, and the dog food in the car. The next morning she'd finish her bag of toiletries, and when Sidra arrived, off they would go. She knew to where, but she hadn't a clue as to why.

By midnight, she dropped into bed so keyed up she might as well have stayed up for all the sleep she expected to get. Jenkins crawled in beside her, snuggled close, and the two lay there for the longest.

Sawyer's questions kept running through her head, and then Maxx' news about the houses. Why in the world would her parents—her mother, at least—not tell her about this property, owned by her family for generations? "It's property, for Christ's sake," she said.

When both she and the dog let out a loud sigh at the same time, she whispered, "You're not sleeping either, are you, baby?" Jenkins' tail flapped the bed. Belle rolled over facing the dog and rubbed her hands through her soft fur until they both fell asleep.

Chapter Five

Everyone needed a Slider, a dog who loved unconditionally and that now waited at the top of the front porch steps, locked outside by Annie and King Cat. Sidra gave him a warm nuzzle, and they walked over to the porch swing. She settled in, and he snuggled close, resting his head in her lap.

"So the old girl locked you out again, huh?" She scrubbed her fingers into his curly red coat. "I hope she gave you something to eat." He looked satisfied, so she interpreted that as a yes. "Sorry, fellow, the trip to Houston took much longer than expected."

The house looked dark inside. Annie always turned out every stinking light in the house before retiring, and she retired at sunset, earlier sometimes. Good thing Sidra kept a flashlight in her purse. She pulled it out, along with her cell phone, and noticed Ben had called several times. He'd been in court all day.

What would he think about her heading off with the rich preacher's daughter to go check out the mysterious ownership of even more mysterious houses in a town known not only for their lakes and waterways but also for their mineral springs and horse races?

She looked down at her best friend. "Guess what, Slider, I am now on retainer—a handsome retainer, if I do say so myself."

Slider licked her hand in approval.

"Yeah, yeah, I know. You're hoping I'll make enough for us to get our own place, don't you?"

The dog whined his agreement.

"Thing is, babe, Annie is getting up there in age, and I'm not sure I'd be comfortable with her living in this big old house all by herself. She could fall or something and…"

Slider let out a groan, like he understood that fact, but didn't have to like it.

"Brings up the question of what to do with you when Belle and I go out of town. A day trip is one thing, but I'm not sure how long this will take, maybe a couple of weeks or so. Perhaps Ben might be free to let you bunk at his house. You think?"

He whined and snuggled closer.

"I know, sweetheart, but you like Ben. I'll come home as quickly as I can."

Curious about their destination, she headed inside, Slider at her heels. After she booked two rooms in Hot Springs, she noticed the note from Annie on the corner of her desk.

"No wonder the house is so quiet. No Annie and no King Cat. I guess I don't need to worry about the old-woman after all." She rubbed Slider's head. "Did she tell you she and Boo Murphy are off on a last-minute Caribbean cruise?" Boo was an irascible old woman who lived on the edge of the swamp. For reasons Sidra couldn't quite understand, she and Annie had become fast friends.

Slider's quizzical expression let her know no one ever told him anything. "All I can say is I sure feel sorry for the sea captain and crew. Those two? Go figure, eh? At least she says she forwarded the office calls to the house since she'll be *unavailable*—Sidra bracketed the last word.

The cruise eliminated Annie from Slider's care. Hopefully, Ben was available. When he didn't answer her phone call, she checked her voice mail.

"Hey babe," his deep, resonant—sexy—voice crooned. "My daughter called. She's in the hospital about to give birth to my first grandson. I'm heading there. Be home in a couple of weeks. Call me."

Chapter Six

Belle's suitcases and the dog's kennel were on the front steps of the mansion when Sidra drove through the *black pearly gates*. Soon, they had the Navigator loaded. Sidra volunteered to take the first shift and slid behind the wheel. It took another hour to get out of Houston.

"Thank you for understanding about my need to bring Slider," Sidra said, and then laughed. "He's well-behaved as long as he has a dollop of yogurt on his dog food."

"Yogurt? Really? What a hoot. And I thought Jenkins a picky eater. We can certainly meet that diet requirement." Belle shifted, adjusting her seat belt. "Between you, me, and the two dogs, we shouldn't get bored. Besides, they help distract my nerves. I have to tell you, I really don't feel good about this trip. A foreboding haunted me all night. My poor dog felt it too."

"Tell me about Jenkins," Sidra said, taking a quick

backward glance at the kennels. Jenkins and Slider appeared to have accepted each other right off—at least after their brief sniffing introduction.

"She's a shelter dog I adopted on a whim. Something about her intrigued me from the first moment I saw her. "I've even wondered if Jenkins is Carl Jung, reincarnate." Belle turned and looked at the dog.

Sidra laughed. "Could be. Who knows?"

"Gay, you know?"

"Carl Jung?"

"No! I mean Jenkins." She laughed. "Well, maybe Carl Jung—I don't know. May sound ridiculous, but I truly believe Jenkins is."

"Why is that?"

"Because she has no use for male companions, human or otherwise—except for Slider. They seemed to take to each other right off. However, Jenkins never let my dad get close, and certainly not Sawyer. Can't stand him."

"Sounds like an indication to me." Sidra spotted a patrol car and cut her speed.

Belle paused. "When I told my parents, they almost made me return her to the shelter. My friends all laughed about it, but I didn't. I *get* Jenkins, and Jenkins *gets* me. I'm not gay, but nor have I met a man I trust—who understands me—and doesn't try to convert me to his beliefs or ways of doing things."

Belle paused. "Includes my dad, too," she continued. "Church people never could understand why I didn't let him baptize me—he even swore we'd never see each other again after we died if I didn't. For some reason, it never resonated with me. I've always held this strange feeling we'd know each other in another life, regardless."

"You may be right," Sidra confessed. "I've wondered the same thing."

Belle asked, "Have you ever felt like you were born into the wrong family?"

"Born? Not really. Married into one, yes," Sidra said

with a snort.

"Since I was a kid, I've always felt like in my eagerness to enter this life, I accidentally fell out of the *Storks delivery basket* prematurely, and into the wrong family."

They rode in silence for an hour or so, Sidra allowing Belle time with her thoughts, while hers went rampant.

While Belle slept, they crossed the Texas border and into Arkansas by way of the town *so great they named it twice* the sign read—Texarkana. Sidra had never been to Arkansas, the Natural State, so the cool misty air of late afternoon surprised her. Vaporous clouds hung low over mountaintops, creating a mystical feeling of having entered another world—a world of magic.

Belle stirred, opened her eyes, and stretched. "This must be Arkansas, huh?"

"We crossed the state line a couple of hours ago. Another half hour and we'll be in Hot Springs.

"So, what are your thoughts about this property you inherited?"

"To tell you the truth, I'm mystified. One thing for sure, I won't stop until I have a better idea of why my mother kept the property all these years and kept it secret. What is it that made my father refuse to acknowledge the fact? My guess is he didn't see an opportunity to make money off the sale." She sucked through her teeth. "Or start a church."

"You sound bitter." Sidra put her blinker on and moved to the right for a hell-bent semi driver to pass.

"You're pretty accurate. I'm hoping this trip will help me make sense of my parents. Who they are—were."

Belle's words trailed off. She grew quiet. Sidra caught a quick glance of a young woman lost in her own thoughts.

Sidra had her thoughts, too, confusing thoughts that propelled her into a world she didn't recognize. A knot in her gut told her she and Belle headed into a past best left alone—but at the same time, beckoned their approach.

The highway soon wended deeper into the Ouachita Mountains, and they entered—paradise. The cool misty air of late afternoon surprised her.

It looked like autumn had come in overnight and swished splashes of orange, gold, and red across the mountains and valleys. Belle opened the moon roof and the two watched the late sun do a number on the sky. The cooler temperatures soon erased Houston's oppressive heat from her soul. The winding highway led through hues of hickories, maples, oaks, and hawthorns. Reds, yellows, oranges, and violets—with green pines sprinkled here and there. Although the deciduous trees were settling down for the coming winter, the evergreens stood watch over the whole. The brilliant show seemed designed especially for them.

The drove into town and located the hotel where Sidra had made reservations and pulled into the parking lot. "I'll check us in."

"That's great, thanks. Here's my credit card.

Jenkins and Slider stirred in the rear. Despite all the frequent stops they'd made along the way, both dogs acted eager to stretch their legs.

"Won't be long now, you two. Soon as we get settled, I'll find a park and let you work off pent-up energy. You've both been super travelers."

Jenkins woofed. Slider's tail banged the cage.

Sidra checked them into their rooms, and by the time she returned to the car, Belle had unloaded the bags and the kennels and given the dogs a few minutes to stretch their legs.

Tomorrow—the houses.

Chapter Seven
Miss Fancy

Some people blame us—say we brought it on ourselves, that we are participants in our own abuse. I ask you what choice did we have—did any of us have—but to survive, especially those who drew the short straw, got pissed on by the crazies, the greedy, and the desperate.

"Learn from your experience. Do something different," others scream in judgment—like hell's angels gave any of us a choice. If we had the freedom to learn from our experiences, we'd be Stephen-fucking-Hawking.

Chapter Eight

After a fitful night of women parading through her hotel room dressed in filmy white gowns and trailing heady perfumes, Sidra awoke when the sun slated through the drapes and hit her in the eyes. She pulled on a pair of blue jeans, a shirt and jacket, crammed her feet into her shoes, leashed Slider, and the two went outside—and fell in love. A new cold front moved in overnight and brought an even crisper feel to the morning. Made her want to move to Arkansas.

She noticed a walking trail and headed that way. It led into the mountains—mountains full of clean, fresh air—and then down into a valley surrounded by dense green forest. Steam rose from hot springs on the side of the mysterious mountain the earliest of settlers called Manataka, or so the sign read.

Again, misty vapors shrouded the valley, feathered lush underbrush, and curled upward through tall trees. In places, the vapors joined low clouds and floated up and away into the pink sky. Other times they lay lightly over the ground like a soft blanket or swirled around the bubbling crystal pools. Manataka held a place of strange, mystical beauty.

Everywhere, the sound of trickling water made sensual music as it bathed the bare faces of fractured cliffs and splashed into creeks at the bottom of the mountain. Steaming waters issued from the rock, growing cones of tufa, porous rock covered with exotic mosses cupped in shades of red and orange, all painted the calcareous rock. Particles of silica, washed by the sun, sparkled like millions of diamonds while pyrite fragments seemed to catch fire and glow.

Hesitant to leave its beauty, she returned to the hotel just in time for breakfast. Belle sat in the lobby, waiting for her.

"Good morning. Looks like you got up early. Afraid I slept in. Took me awhile to go to sleep."

"I couldn't resist a walk. It is beautiful this morning. So you were up late, huh?

"Not because I wanted to, but because my cell phone kept ringing. Finally had to answer it."

"Urgent?"

"He thought it was."

"He? Maxx?"

"No, no. Sawyer? I started to ignore it—but figured if I did, he might send out state troopers. I tend to broadcast this independence thing to him, and he worries. I sent him a text instead. He wanted to know if I'd arrived safely. He must have been watching for it, because he replied right back, expressing relief that I was fine, and to please keep him posted." She shrugged. "Said he cares about my safety. Included a postscript saying he was there, if I needed to talk."

After breakfast and exercising the dogs, they headed to the address of the real estate management company Maxx gave them.

Belle led the way inside and stepped up to the reception desk. "Good morning. How are you?"

"I'm great. How about you?" The receptionist matched Belle's cheerful greeting with a smile that welcomed both of them. "I'm Laura. How can I help you?"

"I want to talk to the agent in charge of the property on Court Street."

A chill stomped into the room.

The receptionist stiffened, her warm smile now frozen in place.

"Oh, you must be Miss Anderson. We were sorry to hear about your mother and father's tragic accident."

Sidra had not been expecting that, although she should have. Belle's parents were national celebrities as surely as any top-selling movie stars.

"We figured you might be coming to check on her property. Excuse me; let me get our property manager." She walked down the hall and, within seconds, came back with a tall, attractive woman with long red hair.

"Good morning," the redhead said, extending her hand. "My name is Kaylie. If you don't mind, let's go into the conference room where we can talk."

After a brief conversation and verification that the two were who they said they were, the realtor offered to go with them to see the property or give them the keys to explore on their own. She explained she'd received instruction from Belle's mom to renovate the buildings, electrical wiring, plumbing, and such several years ago, and sent the money to have it done—so although the houses inside were dirty from lack of use, they were in operable condition.

"Houses? How many are there?" Sidra's interest grew.

"There are three houses and an artist studio in the

back. Actually, Court is a short street overlooking downtown. There is only one other house on the street. It sits on the other side of the empty lot next to yours. Locals call the houses the Ladies of the Court."

"That's a weird name to call houses." Confusion clouded Belle's eyes.

"The houses go a long way back and bring quite a history with them. I can go with you if you like."

"I appreciate your offer, but I'm sure we can find them," Belle said. "We will be back in touch."

Without warning, Warren Chadwick, Sidra's deceased brother, flashed in front of her sporting a big smile. *You got this, Sis,* he whispered.

Once outside, Belle handed Sidra the key fob. "I hope you don't mind, but I'm shaking all over—not in any condition to drive. Would you mind?"

"Not at all. Let's just assume I'm driving until you tell me otherwise." Sidra got inside, set the GPS, and pulled out of the parking lot.

North on Central Avenue, they passed the racetrack and gaming center, busy this time of year. Horse races ran from April to December—another month or so to go.

Down the street another mile, they passed the large white First Baptist Church, hotels and restaurants, another church, and a duck tours bus. After another mile or two and they entered the historic downtown district.

Left on Reserve…and… Where were those houses? Sidra shot a glance over at Belle. *Mesmerized* was the only word that could describe the look on Belle's face.

Sidra turned left and eased the vehicle up the hill.

What the hell do you think you're doing?

Sidra slammed on the brakes and waited for impact. When none came, she checked her mirror relieved to see their car was the only one on the short street.

"You okay?" She glanced over at Belle. "Sorry about that."

Damn, Warren. Scare me to death. You know what

I'm doing. Let me do it without getting in my face.

Belle's attention stayed glued up the hill in front of them. Sidra eased off the brake and nudged the gas pedal. The car didn't seem any more eager to go than she did.

However, at the top of the hill stood three narrow, gaudy, pastel-colored Victorian-style homes looking out over the city as though sentinels on eternal guard.

"Those couldn't be Mom's. I swear they look like whorehouses, No wonder Mother—no, Daddy, acted like they didn't exist."

The same thoughts ran through Sidra's mind, but she halted them halfway. "Let's not jump to conclusions. Hopefully, they look that way because…maybe they were…" She ran out of words to finish the sentence. She eased up Reserve Street, which came to a dead-end and turned into another dead end on the left. Court Street.

The houses, now on their right, perched near the top of the hill. The narrow front yards stopped at a concrete-reinforced wall at street level. The narrow street left no room to park. However, few cars likely drove up the street since the three houses were empty and the large two-story old home across from the empty lot looked abandoned as well. Sidra slowed and drove beyond the houses to a steep driveway on the far side.

"Oh, look, this driveway must be private parking for the houses." She eased into the area and parked.

The two stared at the houses for what seemed an eternity, but likely less than a couple of minutes. Sidra waited on Belle, giving her time to absorb what she saw— and what she imagined. Not to mention the time Sidra needed to reclaim any courage she might locate.

Belle sighed, long and loud. "Do you feel what I feel?"

"Probably. Would you like me to go first?" The aura of the houses left a vague sense of discomfort. No more eager to go inside than Belle, Sidra regretted running off her deceased brother. Warren Chadwick had been super-intuitive about these sorts of things, even if he did scare the daylights out of her sometimes.

I am here, sis, right beside you. You can do this. Just pay attention—pay very close attention. The inaudible words settled inside her chest.

Sidra looked at Belle, who stared without blinking. "I'll go check this first one—the realtor said the locks on the other two weren't working. Come on up when you're ready."

Belle shook her head. "No, I'm ready. I won't be but a minute. Got some memories running through my head. I want to see where they lead.

Chapter Nine
Miss Fancy

Rude gawkers.

Will they never leave us rest in peace? Haven't we been victimized enough? How much longer must we suffer the indignities of the curious with their insatiable appetites looking for a piece of the past to put in their pockets like a souvenir from long ago?

Gawkers all. In an earlier time, here in this very town, these obnoxious people could end up in the lake wearing concrete shoes.

Yes, we are old women—spinsters—ancient, really. Yes, the wounds from our past haunt us, wounds that made us old before our time. Still, we stand, proud and tall, for we know the actions of those who lived—live—within our walls do not define us.

Nor do they let us rest.

Who are these who approach? Why? What do they hope to gain from the horrors inflicted within? Haven't my sisters and I suffered enough?

LEAVE US BE

Chapter Ten

Sidra exited the vehicle, swallowed tongue and all—at least it felt like her tongue—either that or her heart's attempt to escape.

She climbed the concrete stairs from the parking lot to the front yard of the first of the three Victorian-style homes. Side by side, all three houses were painted different colors and backed up against a wooded incline. From the outside, they looked in exceptionally attractive condition—fresh paint, lawn maintained.

Good lord, did Avery know his wife spent money on this property? Not money, but evidently a significant dollar amount. It was bound to be her who paid for the upkeep. Avery wouldn't—not if he wanted to pretend they didn't exist, like the lawyer said.

A vacant lot to the left of the first house separated the

three from a large three-story home in somewhat decent repair, but with no evidence of life within.

Each of the three houses overlooked the city, each with small porches on both the first and second levels. From that vantage point, one could see the whole town. It wouldn't be easy to surprise whoever lived in these houses—you could see them coming. All three houses bore intricate gingerbread trim painted contrasting colors. The trim on the first, the yellow one—was a golden ochre trim. The second, a medium turquoise blue, sported a deep purple gingerbread trim, and the third house, on the far right, was a hideous pink with dark blue trim. The second two stood out even more than the first because someone had taken the time and energy to paint the newel posts varying shades of other colors.

Something—or someone—just stumbled over my grave. Sidra's grandmother, long gone from this earth, whispered.

Sidra shivered and pulled her jacket tighter. Why was her grandmother here? What did all this have to do with her?

"Nonsense." She marched up the front steps of the yellow house. Near the door, hung a name plaque made of wood, with beveled edges that matched the color of the house.

Miss Fancy.

So, Miss Fancy! Someone had actually given the house a woman's name? Weird. Did all three houses have names? Curious now, she walked down the steps, crossed the narrow lawn, and stepped onto the porch of the turquoise house.

Miss Lilly.

And the Pepto-Pink house.

Miss Scarlet.

Weird. Why had no one ever torn the buildings down—the lot overlooking the city was bound to be high-value land.

No sooner had she asked herself the question than she found the answer. Another plaque designated them as historical sites. "Oh my lord, that's why her mother never demolished them. She couldn't. Or maybe her mother didn't want them destroyed for other reasons—like an ancestor worked there—or owned them.

Over the years, someone had enclosed the area between Miss Lilly and Miss Scarlet and made what looked like a hallway between them. Belle put her hand up to the glass-topped door and looked inside, all the way to the rear of what appeared to be a large sunroom.

By the time she got back to Miss Fancy, Belle stood on the porch waiting for her.

"These houses are listed in the historic landmark registry." Sidra climbed the steps of Miss Fancy. "That explains why they still stand."

"Oh, boy. Doesn't explain why they look the way they do. Sid, these are something out of a fairy tale."

"That or a horror movie." Sidra held up the key. "Shall I do the honors?"

"Please, yes. I'm shaking so much I don't know if I could get it in the keyhole."

The lock clicked open, but with resistance.

The door creaked on rusty hinges, swinging wide. A blast of cold, stale air hit them in the face.

All color drained from Belle. She gasped. "I don't know if I can do this, Sidra, and I don't know why."

"That's okay. Want to wait here and let me check it first?"

Belle nodded.

Not that she *wanted* to go first, Sidra told herself, but should. She must perform as the consummate professional. At the moment, Sidra wished she were Catholic with prayer beads and Hail Mary's in her arsenal.

She stood straighter. *It is an old house. Of course, it's cold, dank and…sulphuric.*

The small living room displayed dark hardwood floors. The walls were a deep turquoise—deep as in bold and bright. At the far side, askew pocket doors led to a tiny kitchen with a couple of cabinets. The lawyer said the houses were originally built in 1898. She couldn't imagine a house that old still standing, much less relatively livable. She eased into the kitchen. In a closet to her left, she noticed washer/dryer hookups. So modern conveniences were not totally absent. On the right of the kitchen, a narrow, dark staircase wound around to the second floor. A person could wash dishes at the sink and talk to someone on the narrow stairwell.

"You okay in there?" Belle stood at the front door and peered inside. "What do you see?"

"Everything looks harmless so far."

And it did, until Sidra eased up the tiny curved staircase, and into what she could only describe as *sticky* air.

Her heart raced as she stepped into what looked like a parlor to her left. To the right, a red Victorian looking, carpeted bedroom faced the backyard, and in the front, a second bedroom of similar size on the opposite side of the parlor. A door at the back of each bedroom led to an updated Jack and Jill bathroom with a large soaker tub.

A sadness, not hers, inched tighter around her chest, like events of the past left negative vibrations behind. Hoping to shake the feeling, she hurried downstairs and out to where Belle waited.

"So? What do you think?"

"Not sure what to think, actually," Sid said. "Still trying to figure it out. Let's take a peek in the windows of the other two houses."

They headed down the yellow steps and up onto the porch of the turquoise house, now connected to the pink. Both women held their hands up to the window of the connecting door and saw a long, fairly wide hall leading to the back sunroom.

"These houses have certainly raised my curiosity even more than before. They aren't bad. I could even have them refurbished and use them as a vacation home. I could have house parties, or… I don't know, get-togethers, you know—maybe during racing season. Oaklawn has a good record of racing winners."

Not until she understood something intangible happening behind these walls, Sidra thought.

"I could live in Miss Lilly, and… No, on second thought, it would have to be Miss Scarlet—to piss off my dad. Wouldn't he have loved that?" She laughed, but after a couple of minutes, she took it back. "That sounded mean, didn't it? Guess I still have unpacked baggage with him."

Sidra remained quiet.

"In the meantime, there must be a cleaning team I can get to clean the first house—Miss Lilly. It looked fairly livable to me. What do you think?"

"Everything is coated in dust, but not bad, really." Sidra hated to discourage the excitement Belle felt. A project like this might be what she needed to heal, and to find herself. "You'd need to new appliances, but otherwise—yeah, that sounds like something that might be good for you. Sure won't hurt to give it a go. Sounds like you can afford it. Become a hermit for a while. There aren't any other neighbors on the hill, so you'd have all the privacy you wanted, and the city looks like it would be fun to explore."

"Can I talk you and Slider into staying here with me—at least till I get things going?"

"Oh, wow."

"For a while, of course, and you would stay on retainer—all expenses paid, besides. When you get ready to go home, either I would take you or pay airfare."

Sidra rubbed the back of her neck while thoughts of the possibility clicked in her mind. What it would take for her to do so. An extended retainer—especially at the rate Belle paid, would certainly help her build a bank account. Annie's recent jaunt into parts unknown showed she didn't need babysitting—or if she did, she wouldn't accept any. Slider was here with her. Ben. He might not like her being gone so long, but he'd be fine.

"With three houses, it looks like there would be enough room for both of us and the dogs," Sidra processed the idea out loud. "Not sure what it would be like sleeping here. I have a feeling we'd have more *company* than we want."

"I'm game if you are. Nothing ventured—nothing gained." Belle smiled. "Besides, if you don't stay with me, I am not sure I'll ever get to the bottom of this."

"What about your job?"

"I'll call and tell her I'm taking an extended leave. She'll understand."

"Why don't we try this—let's take it one step at the time," Sidra said, hesitancy in her voice. These houses hooked her, but also scared her to death. Something had happened here—and whatever it was, left energy—energies—behind. What kind, she hadn't a clue. But somehow, she knew if she and Belle stayed, they would not be alone. Thank goodness they brought the dogs. They provided a certain level of protection and watch care.

"Okay. I'm willing to give it a shot—for now. If we run into more than we can handle, we'll know when to leave."

"More than we can handle? What do you mean? Like remodeling?"

"Not quite, and I have no idea at this point. A feeling.

"You think the houses are haunted?"

Sidra shrugged. "I've never seen a ghost before, but if there's something left behind, I guess we can always call Ghostbusters."

Belle sputtered with laughter. "Yeah, the new Ghostbusters—the women!"

Sidra laughed in agreement. "Okay, what's next? Where do you want to start?"

"Got any suggestions?"

"Why don't we drive around and check out the town, pick up cleaning supplies, and take it from there?" Sidra knew she sounded more confident than she felt. "I think we're going to have to feel our way through this. Never had houses for clients before."

After lunch, they stopped by the Hot Springs National Park museum downtown and watched the video about Hot Springs history. They learned of the earliest inhabitants and of their respect for the area. Warring tribes agreed the valley was a place of peace, not a place of war. They called it the Valley of Vapors because of the mists created by the hot springs air mixing with colder.

Next, they learned about the mob's presence during the first half of the 1900s. Al Capone, Owney Madden, and others often frequented the bathhouses to treat ailments, such as syphilis, arthritis, and rheumatism. They followed the old way—Hot Springs served as a place of peace for them as well. Next, they learned the depth of the town's baseball history. How it gave birth to baseball spring training.

The famous Army Navy Hospital—good lord, it went on and on. Fascinating—made her glad she'd decided to stay a little longer. She needed a change as much as Belle. Later, she'd call Ben and let him know of her extended plan.

She and Belle strolled Bathhouse Row, visited one of the hot springs, so hot they could not keep their hands in it. Next, they crossed the street to the famous—infamous Arlington Hotel.

Inside the lobby, they learned of its history—popular during the 1900s. Al Capone, they learned, visited often, and reserved the whole fourth floor all for himself. History reports he walked the streets in complete safety, supported by local authorities on the take.

They rode back through downtown, stopped in the national park headquarters and toured the building, learning the earliest inhabitants were various Native American tribes, of course, and apparently were the first to discover the thermal springs. The tribes held the springs and the valley of vapors sacred.

After that, they strolled both sides of the street and learned more about the mob, the rich baseball history, learned the town was the home of spring training. The sign outside The Ohio Club, listed famous people who'd frequented their establishment since it opened in 1905—movie stars, gangsters, baseball players.

"I had no idea how fascinating this town is—the rich history—the crystal mines nearby—and a short hours drive to a diamond mine," Belle said.

They stopped by a home improvement store to have extra keys made and to order new appliances, along with a flat-screen television—all in stock and deliverable the next day.

"I guess sometimes it pays—paid—to have a daddy with lots of money—more than he knew what to spend it on." A brief smile crossed Belle's face, but it soon turned into—grief?

Next, a local furniture store offered a small living room sofa, chair, table and lamp, a two-person dining table, and furniture for both bedrooms.

"After we get the appliances and furniture in tomorrow, we can go grocery shopping and pick up a few supplies."

"In the meantime," Sidra said as they climbed in the car, "we better pick up cleaning supplies. You and I have a job on our hands." She wondered how much housecleaning Belle had done in her short life. "We've got a butt-load of new furniture coming tomorrow. We need to get Fancy cleaned this afternoon."

"Oh my gosh, you're right."

"And in the process, we better purchase scented candles to help with the closed-up odor. We sure can't open the windows in that old house. Thank goodness the realtor kept the electricity on. Fancy has mini blinds; so if it's okay with you, we won't worry about window coverage for now, but—"

No sooner had Belle started the engine than her cell phone rang over the car's Bluetooth system.

"Excuse me, it's Sawyer. She punched the Answer button. "Hello, Sawyer."

"Hey, babe, checking to see if you're okay." His voice crackled over the phone.

"Better than okay. I've fallen in love."

"What? With whom?"

Belle mouthed to Sidra, "Whom—he's always so correct."

"My property here—the town, the town's rich history."

"So when are you coming home?" Sawyer's strident voice sounded anxious.

When she didn't answer, he said, "You are coming home, aren't you?"

"Sure—in a few days—maybe in a week or so."

"You're staying that long?"

"Actually, I've decided I'm going to fix up these houses. Guess when they were built?

"No clue."

"1898, Sawyer—think of the history they've seen. No wonder my mother wouldn't sell them. They are so quaint—small but big enough."

"What about us?"

Belle shrugged in answer. Too bad the guy on the other end did not see what Sidra saw. If he had, he wouldn't have asked.

"Are you there?" Sawyer asked.

"I'm here. Just…"

He cleared his throat.

"I need this time alone, Sawyer. I have to figure out who I am—what I stand for—in contrast to what I've always been taught."

"I don't understand, I thought—"

"You thought I totally agreed with my parents? Surely you didn't think that."

"Well—no, but… All your friends are here, sweetheart. Everyone has been asking about you, and I don't know what to tell them."

"Tell them I've taken time off that I need…hell, I don't care what you tell them."

"I really wish you wouldn't—"

"What? Say hell? Oh, Sawyer—you are more like my father than he was." She eased the vehicle up the hill and parked in their driveway.

"And I'm supposed to apologize for that?" Sawyer's words blasted over the speaker.

"Okay, this conversation is over. I'm ringing off now," Belle punched the hang-up button, exited the car, slammed the door, and made it as far as Miss Lilly's front steps. She flopped on the first step. Her heads sagged. Her shoulders shook.

Sidra eased beside her and rubbed her back. "It's okay, Belle. Let it out. You're safe. No one is here but you and me."

But were they? Something about Sidra's words felt false. Like they were not as alone as she thought—hoped.

"I can't go back to Houston, Sidra. I'd die there. Everyone in the city recognizes my name and has certain expectations for how I should behave." She burst into tears again. "I'm not my dad, and I'm not my mom either—that is if I knew who the hell she was. That's why I have to learn more about these houses. Where did they come from? How did my mother happen to own them? Who built them, and…?"

"Only way I know to learn," Sidra said in a softer tone, "is we must step it out, one step at the time. Once we get the house livable, we can start digging up their history." She knew that curiosity had killed the cat. She hoped her curiosity didn't accomplish that goal.

Over the next couple of days, Jenkins and Slider spent much of their days getting better acquainted by exploring the wooded hill behind the houses. Jenkins might not like males, but Slider seemed to be her one exception.

Sidra and Belle scrubbed Fancy, Belle upstairs, and Sidra down. Sidra grew more and more curious about the houses, the names, who named them and why. The lady at the historical society had said local legend told how the houses were built for three sisters, and the young women's parents lived in a house next door.

Sidra stopped sweeping and looked up to see Belle coming downstairs.

"You know, I've been thinking," Sidra said, "if these houses were built for those three sisters, you think that might be how they got their names—after each daughter?"

"I could buy how Miss Lilly got hers," Belle said, "but Miss Scarlet and Miss Fancy? What man would allow his daughters such names—sounds more like names of prostitutes—barmaids of the old west." The words had no sooner left her mouth than she stopped dead center of the small dining room. "What if—"

"They were houses of ill-repute?" Sidra finished the question.

"Exactly my thoughts," Belle's eyes grew wide. "Was that why my dad refused to have anything to do with the property—because of their past? Sounds like something he'd do—always so high and mighty—and perfect—at least outwardly. I knew things about him that neither his parishioners nor the world knew. I knew his secrets, at least a lot of them."

"Wow." Sidra realized her mouth dropped open. She shut it.

"It pays to keep eyes and ears open, to listen…maybe my father had a Fancy in his life. I knew of a Chuck. Go figure—Chuck." Belle grew silent, lost in her own thoughts.

In all her life, Sidra had never given prostitution much thought—had no clue where she stood on the subject or the profession. "What constitutes prostitution, anyway," Sidra said. "Does prostituting one's integrity equate to the same?"

"If it does, what did that make my mom and so many other women who were members of his congregation?" She paused. "Shame on me," Belle said. "There I go judging people the same way I hate it when they judge me."

"It's tough to learn to be who we are and let others do the same. I know after I left Sam, I struggled with it. Still do. It's a process, sweetheart."

A large shadow loomed into the room from the open doorway behind them. Startled, they both swung to face a stranger.

"Sorry to startle you, ladies, I'm the locksmith here to repair the locks on the doors of the other two houses. I'll let you know when I'm finished." He tipped his baseball cap and walked off the porch.

Exhausted, filthy, and now weak-kneed, Sidra suggested she and Belle take a break, go outside, and explore the property. Jenkins and Slider hurried along beside them.

The narrow backyard stretched the width of the houses and extended uphill, a marvelous place to escape, to sit in the shade and enjoy Mother Nature at her finest.

After a few minutes, Belle headed inside, Jenkins following her, while Sidra and Slider remained behind, enjoying the crisp fall air whispering through the boughs of nearby pine trees. A pinecone dropped at her feet. She picked it up and examined the spiral of its spines, a perfect Fibonacci sequence, much like the rose and sunflower. A symbolism of enlightenment—the seat of the soul, her late brother Warren Chadwick taught her—attempting to explain his decision for naming his detective business The Third Eye.

Without warning, goosies raged from the middle of Sidra's forehead, across her skull, down her neck, across her shoulders and on to the fingers that clasped the pinecone. The sense that enveloped her felt like something—or someone—waited to get her alone, to assure her that she and Belle were meant to be right there at that very moment in time.

Clueless to where the path would lead, that *something* told her it would lead both of them to where they were meant to go.

Why her? What did she have in common with Belle—other than a subversive religion? Without a doubt, they had been connected over time, somehow or the other.

However, to learn the why and what required Sidra step it out—not only for Belle, but for herself as well.

She turned to see a wrinkled old woman hobbling across the vacant lot. As she grew closer, Slider ambled over to her, tail between his legs, ears down.

"Hello, boy, nice to see you again." The old woman said, her voice scratchy, hoarse sounding. She patted the red curly hair on his head. With that, he seemed to relax, let his tail wag, albeit, slowly.

Her hair, black as midnight, looked matted, her clothes ragged, but clean. "You looking to buy these houses or something? Lots of people rented them over the years, put up businesses, but nothing ever lasted too long."

"Why is that, your think?"

"Oh, I don't think, missy, I know—"

"Really? Why?"

"Times not right yet. You'll know when it is. You come ask me then. Won't do no good for me to tell you now, you wouldn't believe me."

"So are they haunted or something?"

The crone flapped her hand. "Haunted shmaunted—people don't even know what that word means. Maybe they is and maybe they ain't. Don't believe everything you hear, and for sure, don't trust everything you see."

"Then, how in the world?"

"Trust me, White. You come see me when you know for sure the time's right."

"White? No, you must have me confused with someone else. My name is Sidra, Sidra Smart."

"Then your mammy and your pappy named you wrong, your name's White.

Sidra chuckled and ran her hands through her long, white hair.

"And it ain't 'cause of that white mop of hair you got on top of your head, either, if that's what you're thinking."

"Then—?"

"Never you mind..." She flapped her hand and turned to leave.

"Wait, you didn't tell me your name. How can I ask you if I don't know who to ask for and where you live? Do you live in that big house?" Sidra pointed to the only other house on the short, dead-end street.

"Over there," she gave a vague indication of direction, "But I reckon when you're ready, you'll find me."

Sidra glanced from Slider, who lay at the old woman's dirty-sandal clad feet, to the three painted houses, about to ask another question, but when she turned back to where the old woman had stood, she heard only a whisper of wind.

Somewhat shaken, and yet unsure why, Sidra told herself the old woman looked friendly enough.

However, why did the encounter leave Sidra uneasy?

What was the woman's name?

Chapter Eleven

Belle returned to scrubbing, and as she did, thoughts of her mom crept into her thoughts. Why had she never mentioned these houses to Belle? Why had her father refused to acknowledge the property? Both of them acted outgoing when in public, but no one knew who they really were—they kept that part to themselves. Oh, people thought they were authentic, open, honest, giving—that persona had been well cultivated.

Belle knew better. Take the houses, for instance. Why would they handle their inheritance in such a secretive manner? Why not tell her about them, especially since they would be hers one day? Why make her fight to find the answers?

The faster the questions raged, the faster she cleaned. The hardwood floors soon looked almost like new. Belle stood back and admired the healthy shine her work produced.

She never recalled seeing her mother clean anything—except herself. That effort consumed her time and pocketbook. Closets overflowed with dresses of every color. Her mother guarded her figure as closely as her father guarded his bank account. They always employed full-time, live-in help, and with the size of the mansion, several.

Her parents had been so busy winning the world to Jesus, Belle spent most of her growing years with a hired companion. At first, a nanny, but as she grew older, companions. The last one, Maxine, remained on the payroll until after Belle turned twenty-one and she fired the woman herself.

Throughout the day, Sawyer kept calling. Instead of answering, a couple of times she'd texted him. Said she was fine, getting her hands dirty for the first time in her life. Amazed at how good it felt to create clean, shiny surfaces.

Furniture and appliances delivered, house cleaned, and everything arranged, they awoke to an early cold front. Unable to resist the mountain air, Belle strolled around the front yard pulling first one weed and then another until it soon became a serious business. Despite the cooler temperature, she'd worked up a sweat. Out of the corner of her eye, she noticed Jenkins race around from the backyard. "Staking out your territory, huh girl?"

Then she noticed Jenkins wasn't looking at her, but behind her. The dog backed up, teeth bared, with a low growl in the back of her throat. Then she whined, tucked her tail, and ran off. "Some watchdog you are," Belle said, laughing.

"You a movin' in here, are ya?"

Startled, Belle grabbed the porch rail "Wow. I didn't hear you come up."

An old man with wrinkles-on-top-of-wrinkles wore a loose-fitting black cloak and carried a cane. "Right, sorry to scare you, ma'am. Just trying to be neighborly." He indicated the empty boxes in the dumpster and the weeds piled in the barrel.

After catching her breath, she said, "Yes, we've moved in, at least for a while. I recently inherited the property."

"Somebody die?"

"My parents. Seems my mother owned this property, but I don't think my father ever came here. Not absolutely sure my mother did. Kind of weird, don't you think?"

"Oh, I reckon she saw them all right. That's why she ain't never come back. These houses got a history, you know."

"They must. Built in the late 1800s—I'd call that history."

He grimaced, shook his head, and mumbled something about that not being the half of it.

She watched him hobble off then disappear like she'd never seen him. Made her wonder if he'd been there at all, or if her mind played tricks. That was odd. The man seemed nice enough, but… Oh well, old houses always garner reputations.

In time, a pile of weeds filled the trashcan, and her back ached. She stood and purveyed downtown Hot Springs. One thing about the location of her mom's houses, no one could approach from below without notice.

Weary, she grabbed her water bottle and climbed the hill behind the house, chose the shade of a large oak tree, and flopped on the ground to catch her breath. A cool breeze rustled the leaves, and the peaceful morning lulled her into a peace she hadn't felt for a long time.

"I'll teach you to lie and steal, you hideous bastard!"

Belle jumped to her feet, heart pounding, unsure

whether the words or the screams came first, or from what direction.

Everything looked and sounded the same.

Jenkins came running to check on her, hackles up. She whined and nudged Belle. "It's okay, sweetheart. I must have been dreaming. Where's your buddy Slider? You two must have enjoyed exploring, look at all these leaves you brought back with you." She picked through the dog's ginger-colored fur.

Sidra called from the front yard, "Hey, Belle, where are you? I'm hungry! Let's go get lunch."

"I'm in the backyard. Be right there."

Should she mention the encounter under the tree to Sidra?

No. Later. Maybe.

Chapter Twelve

"I'm thinking it's time we moved into Fancy. What do you think?" Sidra put down the menu and stole a quick glance Belle's way.

All color drained from Belle's face. Her eyes stretched wide. "You really think we should? You think we're ready? We still haven't gotten inside the other two houses. I was sort of hoping we could wait, get all three of them ready before we…"

"We could, but that seems to be delaying the inevitable. If we are ever going to get down to the history behind your mother's secrets, I feel like we need to be there—in them—at least in one. The others look like exact models—except for that connecting walkway between them in front and that glassed-in porch across the back. By the way, the locksmith said he couldn't get the locks open, that he needed another tool, and he'd be back."

"I need to call him again—or someone else who might…"

Her voice trailed off as the server brought their food and refilled their glasses of tea.

When Belle didn't resume the conversation, Sidra nudged. "Why don't we move in tomorrow, get the dogs settled, and then we can really dig into their history."

"If you think we should, okay. I know Jenkins will be happier. The two in the house together might be a challenge, but—"

"You want the front bedroom or the one in the back?" Sidra sipped her tea and watched Belle's reaction. She claimed she wanted to know the secret behind the houses, but her actions left Sidra doubting how badly she wanted to know. Eager anticipation to move in didn't run through Sidra's veins either, but she had to push the envelope if they expected to get anywhere.

"The back bedroom. Definitely."

Weary of hotel living, Sidra had no difficulty getting up early, packing her bags, and heading downstairs for breakfast.

Belle sat at a corner table, nibbling on a muffin. Sidra pulled out a chair across from her. "Good morning. You beat me to breakfast. Does that mean you are eager to move into your new home?"

"Ha. Didn't sleep a wink. Figured I might as well get this next step over."

"You packed and loaded?"

"Mmmhmm," Belle indicated, her mouth full of food.

"I'm packed, too. After we finish here, won't take me but a minute to put my bags in the car. Slider's eager to go. He knew something was up the minute I started packing."

"I've already checked both of us out. Just leave your

key in the room." Belle finished her coffee and waited for Sidra.

The hostess stopped by their table with a carafe. The nametag on her uniform said, Cindy. Pretty, in a small town kind of way, with a don't-mess-with-me manner, and long blonde hair restrained in a low ponytail. "More coffee?" she asked and refilled their cups. "You two ladies have been here several days. Are you on vacation or moving here to…?" Her words trailed off.

"Yes and no," Belle said. "I inherited property here, and we came to check on them."

"Them? Not a house but houses?"

"Yes, there are three houses. Mostly abandoned, but still livable."

"Three? Oh, that's nice; what part of town, that is if you don't mind me asking? I've lived here my whole life, sold real estate for a while, but nearly starved to death doing that. I work here in the mornings, then at the home improvement store at the mall in the afternoons—so there ain't too many houses I ain't been in or unloaded building materials for."

Whew, finally, a period. Sidra wondered if Belle would continue the conversation. She did, evidently in no hurry to leave.

"The three houses sit side by side, downtown, just up the hill from Central Avenue."

"You're not talking about the Painted Ladies, are you?" Cindy pulled up a chair and sat.

"The what?"

"Painted Ladies—that's what folks in town call them, that or Ladies of the Court. Are you sure you want to go there? They're haunted, you know."

"Haunted? As in—"

"Ghosts."

"How do you know—you been in them?"

"I been in 'em, sure, showing them to renters. I ain't seen any ghosts, but I hear others have. Besides, the whole town knows. They're on the Haunted Ghosts Tour."

Belle shoved her chair, stood, and headed to the registration desk. Sidra went after her, leaving Cindy alone at the table.

"You mean you don't have a single room open tonight?" Belle asked the hotel clerk as Sidra stepped up behind her.

"We are booked solid for the next two weeks. Racing season and all. I hear all the hotels in town are booked, too. Of course, there's always the chance of a cancelation."

Belle turned around so fast she ran smack into Sidra. "I can't stay there, Sidra," she said. "I can't stay in that house."

"Ghosts, shmosts." Sidra laughed, but inside she hoped not to experience such an encounter. "You going to let a little ghost tale scare you away?

"Come on, we need to stop by the grocery store to get a few things for dinner tonight, and breakfast in the morning, then we'll show those ghosts who's boss," she joked.

After a stop at the market, Sidra and Belle headed to Fancy, bags, dogs, and all. Reminded her of The Beverly Hillbilly's meets Ghostbusters.

The day went surprising well. Sidra and Belle settled into their respective rooms, Sidra in the front and Belle in rear bedroom. Less access—for ghosts, Sidra guessed.

However, the ghosts she'd heard about held no respect for the privacy of others—walls, doors, or otherwise.

After a day filled with unpacking, rearranging furniture, calling another locksmith to replace the lock on the houses next door, locating enough electrical outlets for all of their cell phones, computers, and tablets, or identifying where to add them later, the two dropped into their beds before ten p.m.

Exhausted, Sidra crawled under the covers, and Slider soon joined her, insisting he sleep with a pillow under his head. It took a while before Sidra convinced him he needed his own, rather than hers. They both fell into a coma as soon as they got the pillow situation settled.

Something in the darkness roused her from a deep sleep. What was it? She listened, ears attuned to the nuances of the night. Nothing. She glanced at Slider, now comatose.

She peeled back the covers, slipped out of bed, and into housecoat and tennis shoes. Ears attuned to the sounds of the house, and hearing nothing unusual, she slipped over, grabbed the doorknob to the balcony off her bedroom. The door opened with only the slightest creak.

The night air sent a shiver through her. She pulled the robe tighter. The long curved-fingernail moon overhead added little illumination to the night sky. The dimmed lights from downtown Hot Springs glowed softly in the distance. The night around her seemed black as pitch—until she turned to her left—towards Miss Lilly and Miss Scarlet. A quick small light emanated from Scarlet's front window. It flickered and went off, leaving the softest ember glow behind, then another, and another.

Had that been what awakened her? How in God's name could it, and how could anyone be inside? The locksmith hadn't been able to get the lock off the door—several locksmiths, to be accurate.

Now what? Did she call the police? What could possibly be in those houses that anyone would want to steal?

She crept back inside, pulled a jacket over her robe, tucked a flashlight and her Glock in the pocket, and returned to the balcony. The stairs led down the side of the house towards the rear.

At the bottom, she circled to the front yard. Sure enough, the lights still glowed in slow movement, first fast, then slow…almost…inviting.

Sidra kept her sights on the flickers while she made her way across the uneven yard. She dared not turn on her light. She knew she couldn't get inside the house, but she might look through the windows. As she drew closer, she slipped her hand into her pocket and tightened it around the gun. In a moment of panic, she questioned if she had reloaded the clip?

She eased up Miss Lilly's porch steps and peered through the window.

Women dressed in loose-fitting see-through gowns reclined on Victorian-looking red velvet sofas and chairs. Each held glowing cigarettes between ruby red lips or dangled them from fingers with bright red nails. Rouged cheeks and long tousled hair matched styles from another era. Although they appeared to be laughing and talking, Sidra heard only the sound of her own labored breathing and a pounding heart.

How had these women gotten inside? And where had all the furniture come from? When she looked earlier, the room had been totally bare. Dare she call the police?

They won't see what you see, Sidra.

Thanks a lot.

She tried the doorknob, surprised when the door swung open—its hinges silent as a Christmas mouse. She stepped inside. The living room stood empty—devoid of furniture, women, lamps, rugs…everything except an odor of cheap perfume and—musk?

What the—? She blinked a couple of times, went back out, and looked through the windows again. There sat the women in repose, the lamps, the furniture, and a black cat.

The same cat she'd seen outside a few days ago. It leapt into the lap of a big blonde, buxom woman, moved around until it found its sweet spot, and then lay and closed its eyes.

Did she imagine they were—or weren't there? Or had she gone crazy?

Give it another try, she told herself.

Okay, she'd try again. At the door, she turned the knob and went inside—nothing.

However, as she gawked and questioned her sanity, she felt a chill cover her whole backside, move all the way through her, and out the front.

She closed her eyes a second, hoping to make sense out of the odd experience.

She opened them to the sight of an older, heavier, bleached-blonde woman in front of her.

Had that been the cold she felt? Did the woman pass through her?

What the hell? Was she going mad? She wished now she'd awakened Slider and brought him—even if she had to drag him across the yard. Her heart pounded so loud she feared the women would spot her and... And what? Were they real? Was she dream walking?

She contemplated the group, still soundlessly chatting and laughing. One older woman carried an air of authority. The Madam? Perhaps.

At last, weariness overtook her and she decided she'd gone flat, slap-dab crazy. She left the porch, hurried across the yard, up the stairs to her room. Once in bed, she snuggled in next Slider. In the morning, she'd check through the front windows of both Miss Lilly and Miss Scarlet.

Should she tell Belle?

Chapter Thirteen

Sidra didn't sleep the rest of the night. At the first hint of daybreak, she went downstairs, let Slider out, and then put on a pot of coffee. Still unsure whether to tell Belle about her experience the night before, Sidra decided if she did, it wouldn't be first thing in the morning.

"I don't know about you, Sidra, but I slept like a baby." Belle and Jenkins bounded around and down the stairwell. "That coffee smells great. Come on, Jenkins, I'll let you outside."

Jenkins hurried to the door, eager, it seemed, to join Slider. Their greetings of mutual sniffs confirmed a bond developing between the dogs.

Sidra fiddled with the handle of her coffee mug and waited till Belle poured a cup and joined her.

"No…no… I can't say I had a restful night." Sidra

squirmed in her chair. She questioned whether or not to tell Belle what she'd witnessed last night. In the light of day, she couldn't be sure she'd seen it. Or dreamed it.

"Sorry to hear that. Anything going on?"

Sidra humpfed. "Not real sure."

"Want to talk about it?"

"Not really—at least not now."

Belle added sugar to her coffee, stirred, and took a big slurp. "Sorry for slurping. My mother would have a fit—she always did—about my delight in my first cup of the day. Seems like that first mouthful tastes better if you slurp."

Sidra smiled. "Doesn't bother me. Slurp myself when I feel like it." Nothing about the morning or the night before left her in a mood to enjoy anything.

"You know what I'd like to do this morning?" Belle asked, seemingly oblivious to Sidra's struggle.

"What's that?"

"I'd like to go downtown for breakfast. I saw a pancake shop just down the street from The Arlington Hotel. I checked online, and the reviews look good. I'd like to try it. The website says they've served pancakes there since 1940."

Food of any kind—even the thought of eating—didn't sit well on Sidra's stomach or any other part of her anatomy at the time, but she shoved that aside. At least a trip to town might help get her mind off the night before, and time to figure out how she planned to tell Belle she'd lost her marbles.

"Sounds good to me," she lied. "What's it called?"

"The Pancake Shop." Belle laughed. "Very creative, don't you think? Has great reviews, though. I read comments by the New York Times, Chicago Tribune, and Southern Living."

By the time they arrived, the restaurant had a waiting line outside the door. After forty-minutes window-shopping the neighboring storefronts, the hostess came out to get them. "Sorry for the wait." She ushered them inside.

"Are you always this busy this time of year?" Belle asked on the way to a table.

"Oh, yes. One thing about Hot Springs, there is always something going on in this town. In October, we have our Hot Springs Documentary Film Festival. You'll see producers and filmmakers from around the world still here." She located their table, invited them to sit, and offered menus.

"Documentary Film Festival? Hadn't heard about it." Belle took the menu. "Is it new?"

"Since 1996. *MovieMaker* magazine recently added it to their global list of top film festivals. How about a mug of fresh hot coffee?"

"Yes, please," they said in unison.

"And a glass of ice water for me, please." If Sidra hydrated, perhaps the hyperactive nerves might find a soft place to settle.

"I know what I want to eat," Belle said, browsing the menu. "I've never eaten Buckwheat pancakes." She gave a snarly laugh. "My mother only allowed low fat, low carb, low sugar, and no taste to ever cross the threshold of our house."

When the server returned for their order, "Buckwheat pancakes with maple syrup, fried eggs, bacon, and hash browns," shot out of Belle's mouth.

"With butter?"

"Oh, yes, lots of butter." Belle grinned up at the server.

Sidra felt queasy. "Dry toast and jam, please." She collected the menus, handed them to the server.

While Belle studied the autographed photos of famous movie stars hanging on the walls around them, Sidra glanced around a room full of what could be filmmakers—not that she knew any—however, snippets of conversations from nearby tables confirmed they most likely were.

A woman who sat across from them kept glancing their way. When she caught Sidra's eye, she pointed to Sidra's socks. "I love your Samhain socks." Her smile looked warm enough to be that of a dear friend.

For the life of her, Sidra couldn't remember putting on socks that morning. A quick check revealed Jack-O-Lanterns and black cats around her ankles. "Thanks. A little late in the season, but I grabbed the pair on top."

"I do that all the time." The woman smiled. "I'm Ravina Nation, by the way. I'm a sculptor and own and operate a bronze foundry out from town a ways. So are you two just visiting, or have you recently moved here?"

"Visiting," Sidra and Belle said in unison.

"A vacation, huh? Hot Springs is a great tourist town. With all the large crystal veins running deep in the earth, you'll find a lot of energy here." She laughed. "History proves that."

"More a business trip," Belle said. "I just inherited family-owned property up the hill off of Reserve Street."

"Court Street?" The woman's mouth gaped open. "You mean, the three—?"

"You know those houses?" Sidra's visit the night before slashed its way behind her eyes.

The woman laughed—but not an amused laugh—more a sense of *knowing*. Her eyes narrowed. "You mean those three row houses at the top of the hill?"

"Yes, those."

With an abrupt change in her demeanor, the woman pushed away from the table. "Nice meeting you. I rather suspect we will run into each other again. Good luck on those houses."

The last thing they saw was her back, exiting the door.

Sidra glanced down at her Halloween socks. She'd never wear them again without thinking of the stranger called Ravina and wondering why the mention of the three houses caused such a weird reaction.

Perhaps she knows something you don't, Warren whispered.

"Perhaps."

"Excuse me?" Belle raised her eyebrows.

Taken aback that she'd spoken the words aloud, Sidra laughed. "Oh, just talking to myself." She tucked Warren's words away to revisit at a later time.

"Why don't we stroll down Bathhouse Row," she suggested, stalling until she knew whether or not to tell Belle about her experience in Miss Lilly the evening before. The seeming comfort of those involved, relaxed, the smell of cigarette smoke, their dresses—what they covered and what they didn't—and most of all, the older blonde bombshell.

They strolled Central Avenue beneath towering Magnolia trees, passed Maxwell Blade's Magic Show, the Oddities and Curiosities Shop, a handmade soap store, numerous art galleries, other restaurants, hotels, and bathhouses.

Sidra caught sight of the old, raven-haired woman who came into their yard and swore Sidra's last name was White. Also swore she knew something about the houses no one else knew—but refused any more talk about the subject. Now, she wore a long-fringed violet-colored wrap clutched to her chest, her black hair fluffing in the breeze. She scurried around sightseers, disappeared inside doorways, only to reappear in another location. No one seemed to notice her—not even Belle. Sidra dared not ask. After last night, she didn't trust anything she saw—let alone her own sense of knowing.

However, when the woman crossed the street right through the middle of moving traffic and made it to the other side without incident, a familiar name caught Sidra's eye. Margaret's. It. offered drinks, music, and food. She'd read about it in a brochure she picked up in the hotel lobby, along with several other places visitors might want to see while visiting Hot Springs National Park.

Follow her, Sid. She's leading you…

Dammit, it Warren…

I said FOLLOW HER. Do you want my help or not?

"No, I don't… Wait…yes…"

"Excuse me?" Belle looked at Sid with raised eyebrows.

"Sorry, I…talk to…myself, sometimes." She had to watch that, else Belle would see how close to *certified* Sidra really was—carrying on a conversation with a dead brother fit a little outside the norm.

"See Margaret's, across the street?" Sidra pointed. "I read where in the mid-1900s the building housed a brothel owned by a woman of the same name. Current owners kept the name of the madam."

"Madam? Really?"

"Seems Hot Springs had quite a thriving prostitution business during the Gangster era."

"What gangsters?"

"Al Capone, Owney Madden, and all the others. Apparently they enjoyed the baths of Hot Springs, and the local officials received a little payola for letting them live in peace while vacationing here."

"How do you know all that?" Belle's mouth formed a perfect O.

"It's my job to know those kinds of things." Sidra laughed.

"Well, I guess that had something to do with my dad's shame over mom's inheritance. Makes me wonder if any of them were related to my mother's family."

"Could be." A sudden flashback of what Sidra witnessed in Miss Lilly the night before began to make sense. It also created more questions than answers. All of that occurred many years ago. Margaret was dead and gone, had been for years, but…

Sidra led the way across the street to Margaret's and

paused to read the historical marker on the corner of the building. Belle stood behind and reading over her shoulder. Sidra glanced in the plate glass window to point out the year on the plaque, but when she looked, it wasn't Belle's reflection she saw. Rather, an older woman stood reading over her shoulder, a blonde-haired, buxom woman.

Meet Margaret.

Shut up Warren, and mind your own damn business.

Sidra spun and nearly toppled into Belle.

"Are you okay?" Belle grabbed Sidra's elbow.

"I'm fine. Just felt a little dizzy. Shall we go inside?"

"Sure, why not."

That early in the morning, no one stood behind the bar, but a few people sat at small round tables chatting, drinking coffee. One man sat near a small platform working on a laptop—absorbed in some kind of project.

Belle stood next to her and grabbed Sidra's forearm in a vise-like grip. "Sidra," she whispered panic-like. "Look at that portrait on the wall."

Sidra glanced at Belle then followed her gaze to said portrait. Sidra recognized that face, those—boobs—that smile—and an aura so strong the artist had captured it on canvas.

Confused, Sidra questioned whether Belle hadn't followed her the night before.

"That woman," Belle pointed, "I'd swear that woman…is…my mother."

Chapter Fourteen

"Your mother? Belle, do you mean— Sidra led Belle to a small table near the windows and ordered two cups of coffee.

Na-na-naa. Told you so.

Put a sock in it, Warren.

"I mean put a wig on that woman, dress her in a modern, high society outfit, take off a few pounds, shrink the boobs, and she could pass for my mother."

Sidra wanted to ask Belle what the hell that meant, but reality had already burrowed through her skin's epidermis, well on its way to the dermis and beyond—or was that Warren? She shivered.

Belle kept glancing at the portrait, and then back at her hands, clasped on the table, knuckles white. Neither said anything for several minutes while the encounter settled deeper into their reality.

An old man walked into the room from a door in the rear. Soon after, a woman walked over and whispered something to him, pointing up at the portrait, and then in a vague gesture, indicated Belle. When they noticed Sidra looking at them, they hurried through the same back door from which the man had come.

"You know, Belle, I think it's time we went home and checked on the dogs, don't you think?"

Nothing.

"Belle?"

Without a word, Belle moved towards the front door. Sidra left cash for the coffee, grabbed their things, and hurried after her. Outside, she took Belle by the arm, led her to the car, and headed home—whatever home was.

She had to tell Belle what she'd seen the night before. She must. Otherwise...well...otherwise...how else could they figure out...figure out...what?

Sidra pulled into the driveway. The dogs lay resting on Fancy's front porch. Belle exited the vehicle before Sidra could push the gear into Park.

Sidra called out to the dogs. "Hey, you two, did you think we'd abandoned you? Still have water?" Sidra checked the outside water dishes, refilled them, and then went inside to find Belle while Jenkins and Slider ran off together on another neighborhood adventure.

Belle was not inside. Sidra went back outside and checked the front yard then went around Fancy to the back.

A magnificent large oak tree, its leaves now a brilliant red, served as a support for a forlorn, confused-looking Belle. Tears left dirt trails down her face. Her eyes were open—staring—like no soul existed behind them.

"Belle? Honey? Are you okay?" Sidra made her way up the slight incline, flopped on the ground beside Belle, and clasped one of her hands. "Honey? Please look at me."

"I have no idea who I am, Sidra." Belle's words failed to bring her back from wherever she'd gone. "How do you find yourself when the foundation underneath you collapses?"

"I don't know, sweetheart, but I know we can find it—together."

They sat in silence for a few minutes, Sidra honoring Belle's need for quiet.

When leaves rustled without cause, Sidra looked up, expecting to see the dogs. Instead, a clean-shaved, immaculately dressed man in black slacks, starched white shirt, black tie, and shoes that shined like glass headed their way.

"May I help you?" Sidra rose to her feet.

"Sawyer?" Belle exclaimed. "What are you doing here? How'd you find us?" Belle scrambled to her feet.

Good questions, Sidra thought, except she added a couple of four-letter words to hers.

By then, Sawyer had rushed over, pulled Belle to her feet, and wrapped his arms around her. Belle's arms did not reciprocate. Instead, she looked like she'd turned into the proverbial pillar of salt.

"What are you doing sitting out here in the dirt? Your clothes are filthy." He brushed leaves off her skirt. "What possessed you to do that?"

"Well, not that it's any of your business, but I was earthing," she yelled.

"Earthing? Not more of that woo-woo stuff is it?"

He grabbed Belle's arm and tugged her towards the front yard.

"Sawyer! Stop it! What the hell do you think you're doing? Let me go!" Belle shoved him away and stomped inside the house.

Sidra followed. "Want me to lock the door on him?" She chuckled.

"Yes, but it wouldn't do any good. Knowing him, he'd just pound on the door."

Within seconds, they heard Jenkins with a *move one muscle and you're dead meat* growl in her throat.

"Belle! Belle! Call off this stupid dog before she attacks me."

"I told you she hated men," Belle laughed, "and Sawyer tops her list."

By then, Slider picked up the cadence, drawing confidence from Jenkins. The cacophony drowned out Sawyer's next words.

"We better do something," Sidra said, peeking out the window, "or we're either going to have the police, the EMS, or the whole town here."

"I'll have to do it. Wouldn't matter to Sawyer who came. He's always in the right.

Belle opened the door, ordered Jenkins to hold strain, and when she did, Slider quieted as well, but with a lift to his head, like he'd conquered the world. The two marched off and around to the rear of the house, but Jenkins retained a low growl, giving notice she wasn't done yet.

Sawyer rushed up the steps and through the front door before the dogs started in again. Sidra moved to close the door against the chilly air when she noticed the wrinkled old man, still wearing the same long black cloak standing in the yard, looking up at her.

Chapter Fifteen

"I still don't know why you had to come check out these houses, Belle. Look at this place." Sawyer swung his arms in an all-inclusive arc. "You've got enough on your hands with your parents...and all. You know what I mean? Come home with me, marry me, and let's continue your father's legacy."

"Legacy? What the hell are you talking about? You mean like—at the church?"

Sawyer grinned and reached for Belle's hand, but she moved it behind her back out of his reach. When she did, he reached for the other—which went behind her, too.

Sidra swore Belle also drew an invisible line between herself and Sawyer.

"A couple of the deacons are talking about me taking over the reins. Lead the church, to pick up the plans your dad laid out before—well, you know—keep the vision on track. You may not know it, but I've worked with him on his next couple of books—co-authored—so to speak. They have encouraged me to continue with his publisher and get the books out there and see how it goes."

"What? No way," Belle's face turned red. "I may not have agreed with my dad, or believe like he did, but one thing I know, your feet aren't big enough to fill the shoes he wore—not only wore but built with his own hands, so to speak."

Sawyer had crossed Belle's invisible line. She looked ready to spit fire.

"Sawyer." Sidra moved between the two. "You're pushing her. She's not ready to deal with this. She's still trying to figure out who her parents were. Until then, you're better off giving her the space she needs. Best you—

Something stopped Sidra mid-sentence… some…*thing* crept—nudged its way under the skin on the back of her neck. She swatted at it, certain a spider tried to take up residence—but nothing. She shuddered.

"If you think you're going to talk me into leaving, Ms. Smart, don't waste your breath. I'm not leaving here without Belle. She doesn't—Belle—you don't need to do all this digging. Sometimes it's best if we don't disturb sleeping dogs. No telling what you'll uncover, and I don't think any of it will make your life better. You don't need to know the past. It's gone. Come back with me."

Something changed—something weird with the guy's body language. What was it? Dark, foreboding, dangerous…even…

"This, this…place…certainly isn't something you need to spend your time resurrecting from the dead. My advice is put a match to it, burn it to the ground. They should have been burned down the same night the other one burned—burned to ashes!"

Sidra starred at Sawyer, bug-eyed. How did he know

about the house next door burning? How did he know anything about this property? Whoa…

Belle fled upstairs, her feet pounding like Sidra's heart.

That left Sid and Sawyer staring at each other.

Dead silence filled the space between them, along with the distaste and anger Sidra felt towards Sawyer.

Sawyer knew more than he should—than anyone would have unless…

Sidra knew it. She took in a slow deep breath before saying, "Sawyer, sit down, let's talk."

"I've said too much already… I… His feet shuffled, he looked over his shoulder at the door as though considering the location of Jenkins in relationship to how long it might take him to get to the car. Then he flopped on the small sofa, head down, arms resting on his legs.

Silence.

Sidra sat across the room and didn't say a word. She knew the power of silence—of not speaking first in awkward situations.

The silence built, while Sawyer looked trapped in his own web.

Upstairs, she heard Belle pacing. Then nothing. Nothing stirred, except the wheels in Sidra's head.

"Tell me," she said.

Sawyer looked caught with no escape plan.

"She's not going to give up until you do. You know that, don't you? She's not stupid, she heard what you said, and like me, she knows there's no way you could have known about there even being a house next door, much less burned down—and at night."

"Sorry, I better leave." He stood and looked out the window. "If I go real quietly, maybe the dog—"

"Maybe you better."

"Tell Belle…"

"Just go. Belle can think whatever she wants. Doubt she'll give it much thought." But Sidra would—lots of thought.

Sawyer eased outside, down the steps, and made it to his car just as Jenkins rounded the house and headed straight for him.

Good lord, if that dog got his teeth into Sawyer, Sidra would never get in the middle.

Relieved she didn't have to make that decision when the car door slammed shut, she turned to see Bella standing in the kitchen. Evidently, she'd seen Sawyer's departure—or heard it.

"Want some tea? I'm making me a cup." Belle turned on the fire under the teakettle and collected tea bags from the tin canister.

"If that's all you're offering," Sidra said, laughing.

They collected their mugs of hot tea and settled at the small kitchen table. Neither said anything for a few minutes. Again, Sidra waited, choosing to allow Belle to lead the conversation.

"None of this makes any sense, Sidra. None of it. I'm more confused than ever and beginning to think I'm living in a crazy world. What is going on? How in the world did Sawyer know where we were and that a house next door burned down over a century ago?"

Sidra chuckled. "It isn't funny, but... You know, I asked myself the same question, and tried to ask your boyfriend—"

"He's not my boyfriend." Belle's elevated pitch could have raised the roof.

"Sorry, sorry." Sidra held up her hands. "I...okay, Sawyer. I tried to get him to sit and visit, hoping to ask him that very question, but I got the idea he hadn't intended to reveal how much he knew—couldn't get out the door fast enough—vicious dogs be damned."

A floodgate opened and broke through Belle's wall, tears streamed, shoulders heaved, and sobs wracked her body.

Sidra sat in silence, relieved Belle grieved her loss,

her devastating loss, regardless of this mess. After a good fifteen minutes that seemed like two hours, Belle lifted her head from the table, wiped her nose, grabbed a handful of tissues nearby, and cleaned up the mess.

While Belle collected herself, sipped her tea, and grabbed more tissues, Sidra decided Belle had experienced enough secrets for a lifetime. Regardless of how much more it might confuse her, Sidra needed to tell her about the night before.

"What?" Belle said, staring across the table at her.

"What, what?"

"Sidra, you know something you're not telling me. Is it about Sawyer? My parents?"

"Not Sawyer—at least not anymore than you know—but, something happened last night I haven't told you about—wasn't sure I wanted to—wasn't sure I believed it myself, but…"

"Don't protect me, Sidra. Tell me. Don't leave out anything."

"Well, something woke me in the middle of the night and…" She described how she'd awoke, was drawn outside and over to Miss Lilly, the glow of cigarette ashes, the sense of…what? How she'd looked in the window and seen the ephemeral women lounging around the room, what they looked like, how they were dressed, how the door opened, and she'd walked inside to an empty room— how everything had disappeared.

Belle listened, staring at Sidra's mouth as she talked—stared at it, actually—but didn't look like she saw anything. Like her mind absorbed what her psyche couldn't.

Sidra waited for Belle to catch up—if possible. Sidra wasn't sure she, herself, was caught up or believed it.

After what seemed like forever, Belle pulled her focus off Sidra's now silent lips to her eyes. "Is that it?"

"Not really. Didn't want to throw too much at once."

"Lay it on me."

Sucking in a deep breath, Sidra began by revisiting their trip to the Pancake House and the woman's odd reaction when she learned of the houses. Then on to the old woman who crossed the street through heavy traffic like the street were empty and led Sidra to Margaret's.

Dare she tell her about Warren and his warnings?

"There's something you don't know about me, Belle."

Belle gave a snarky laugh. "You think I don't know? Remember, I called you."

"Excuse me?"

"Sidra, I am aware you have—shall we say—out-of-the-ordinary gifts?"

Sidra fiddled with the sugar spoon on the table.

"I do my research. I know your brother Warren was an intuitive, and I know he left his business to you. Figured there must be a reason for it."

Sidra thought she'd kept her secret.

"Okay, before you say anything else, I want to hear you, Sidra Smart, lay claim to your psychic gifts. I want you to own them because, for some reason, I get the idea you haven't."

Damn.

The two sat in silence once again.

"I—I don't know if I can—you see—I never knew—"

"Bullshit, Sidra. You knew."

Thoughts ripped through Sidra. She always blamed Sam, her ex-husband, preacher for suppressing what she knew in her gut. Maybe Sam wasn't to blame. Maybe fear kept her from taking a closer look at it—a closer look at what she'd always known—that she knew stuff—felt stuff, and didn't know why, how or what it was. She had ignored the stupid blue flame on her first case, then the lighthouse, and the slave trade—what else had she ignored? Oh yes, Warren's declaration that she shared the gift with him—him and his intuitive investigations. The fact that even from the grave, he kept nudging her in the ribs. She resisted until the divorce—then it boiled down to eating or starving—and thank goodness Aunt Annie moved to town and bought the old colonial style home—haunted, itself—and insisted Sidra live with her.

"Sidra, Sid," Belle's voice brought Sidra to the kitchen table and the mug she squeezed so tight her hands ached.

"Wow, I hit a nerve, didn't I?" Belle put her hand on Sidra's. "You look like scales just fell from your eyes."

Sidra exhaled, as though she'd surfaced from a dive underwater, a dive longer than lungs full of air could handle. "Nothing like being called on the carpet by your client," she said, chuckling.

"I'm sorry. I didn't mean to be disrespectful. It's just… I kept feeling like you—"

"No, no. You were on target. I've denied it a lifetime. Warren knew it, kept telling me, and yes, that's why I inherited the Third Eye, but—"

"But it scared you."

"How did you know?"

Belle's hands cupped Sidra's on the table. "Got a guess?"

"No, not you, too?"

"Why do you think I scared my parents? Scared them to death. They saw it as devil worship. Evil, wicked. I figure Rev. Sam felt the same way about you."

Sidra laughed. "My brother Warren always told me I was clairaudient."

"I sense it, too," Belle said.

The room grew silent.

This time, Sidra broke the silence. "Warren was with us this morning when we were downtown."

"Okay, that settles it," Belle said. "Tonight we pay another visit to Miss Lilly. It isn't too late. We're still under a new moon. That's when I figure they appear."

Relieved the topic moved off Warren's revelations about Margaret and Belle's connections, Sidra decided to wait until after the Miss Lilly visit to share the other tidbit of news.

"Then we better keep the dogs inside. Hate to think what they'd do if they go with us," Sidra said.

"Absolutely not. Those dogs go—both of them," Belle said, resolute. "Tonight, we *all* go pay Miss Lilly a visit, whether she's ready for us or not."

Chapter Sixteen

They waited until midnight. Sidra felt like she'd jump out of her skin if they didn't go soon. She hoped for more moonlight and for the clouds to pass and expose shadows—otherwise, how would they know what they witnessed belonged to them or someone—something else?

The dogs lay on the living room floor with their ears perked and tails still, like some kind of energy floated above them and bounced off the walls to garner their attention.

She looked at Belle—a bronze statue staring off into the distance.

The soft whisper of her own breath filled the gap of silence when her lungs reminded her to breathe.

Belle blinked a couple of times and then, reoriented to time and space, eased to her feet with the speed of a turtle.

Alerted by the movement, the dogs scrambled up, headed to the door, and waited, eagerness activating their tails

"Okay, it's time. You ready, Sid?"

"Me? Oh, yeah, sure, I guess it's now or never—"

"Okay, let's do this. Let's go see if what you saw last night is an every-night occurrence. Or if you see it, but I don't."

"Could be the opposite." Sidra wrapped her jacket tighter. "If I imagined the whole thing, then we have another issue to be concerned about."

"Trust me. You did not imagine it. Don't ask me how I know—I just do. Something about this whole situation tells me we aren't here by accident…or my mother didn't have good reason to keep the houses despite Dad's objections."

They stepped onto the porch, the autumnal night air brisk, invigorating—and eerie enough to bring goosebumps. Miss Lilly looked foreboding, daring an approach. No warm soft glows flickered through the windows like the previous night.

"I don't see a thing." Sidra said, relieved—and disappointed. What if the women weren't there? What if she imagined the whole thing?

"Looks like the dogs don't sense anything." Belle kneeled beside Jenkins and rubbed her head. "Everything look okay, babe?"

Jenkins wagged her tail.

Slider copied her. Funny how Slider seemed to respect Jenkins, look up to her as his leader. Guess he knew strong females when he saw them, even if the female was canine. Then again, pack leaders of their European ancestors were female.

"What time was it last night when something woke you, Sid? I'm thinking we may be too early."

"Two a.m. I remember looking at the clock on my

radio."

"The Witching Hour."

"Excuse me?" Sidra stumbled, grabbing the handrail to steady herself.

Belle laughed. "Not really, just teasing you, but timing is important. There are two sides to the belief about those *in-between times* when the veil between the physical and the spiritual grow thinner. Those who practice black magic believe between three and four a.m. is when witches, ghosts, and demons come out because the Catholic Church doesn't hold Canonical services then. I don't practice black magic."

"Good to know," Sidra said.

"However, there does seem to be stronger energy at certain times and for different people—even locations. Hot Springs, for instance, is a more powerful, *thinner* place by its very nature. The positive energy of the hot mineral springs, the gigantic underlay of crystal veins..."

"So?"

"To be on the safe side, let's avoid three so as not to confuse or disturb anyone...or...*anything*. Let's check again, say, around two."

Sidra tried to suppress a yawn but failed. "Then we better put on the coffee."

They returned to Fancy and soon consumed a whole pot of strong coffee. Of course, the dogs, still wired to go, had no trouble snoozing, confident they'd know when.

They did—at least Slider did. His whine roused Sidra from fireflies and angels wings. Startled, she looked from Belle, also dozing, to the flashing red 2:00 a.m. on the clock.

A few minutes later, they again gathered in the front yard. The air felt different, smelled different. It even tasted different—something stale...raw...musty. The dogs' ears stood on alert—not to mention the hackles on their backs.

A soft glow from Miss Lilly's front window made Sidra grab Belle's elbow. "Look," she whispered. "Did you see that?"

Jenkins took off first, with Slider right behind, at times barking in unison, and others, as an echo.

"You ready?" Belle asked with a quick glance Sidra's way.

"Ready as I'll ever be." The experience the night before had shaken her enough for a lifetime. Maybe she should let Belle go see it by herself. It was bound to have been a dream, else why did the women disappear when Sid went inside—and how in the world did she get the door open in the first place? What caused the glow?

Sid, get your scared butt over to those women. They have been waiting decades for this night. Don't disappoint them.

Damn it, Warren.

Sid wrapped courage around her shoulders and she and Belle tiptoed across the small yard, their feet crunching on layers of red and orange leaves shimmering in the now soft moonlight. Sidra glanced up, half expecting the silhouette of a witch on a broom.

Perhaps the witch was inside the house, disguised as…as…well…

"I see what you mean," Belle said, grabbing Sid's arm. "Look, there's a glow, then it moves. Then…there…"

They stepped up on the porch and peered through the dingy windows. Sure enough, women in elegant poses lounged on red velvet chairs, their long, loose-fitting negligees trailing the floor.

Sidra squeezed Belle's hand. "See, I told you," she whispered as Belle sucked in a deep, audible breath.

"They're here, Sid, just like you said." She tightened her grip on Sid's arm, and still whispering said, "Look, they appear to be talking and laughing, but—oh my God, I don't hear a word. Do you?"

"Not a sound, and didn't the other night, either." At least she wasn't crazy.

Belle reached for the doorknob. "And you said the

door wasn't locked—or at least it opened for you." She twisted the knob, and the century-old door swung open on rusty hinges but without the slightest sound—except the wafting roar of heady perfume.

"What's that smell?" Belle looked over her shoulder at Sidra.

"My grandmother wore it all the time—it's *Evening in Paris.*

"*JCMM!*"

"What?"

"Jesus Christ Mary Magdalene—just an expression—the closest I could get to swearing in earshot of my parents," Belle whispered. "Where are the dogs? What are they doing?"

Sidra found them—still in the yard, hackles raised. She motioned them to come, but they stood steadfast, frozen in place."

"Never mind. Let's go in."

"You can see them out here, but when you get inside, they won't be there. I promise. Been there done that."

Belle shrugged and took a step forward. Sidra waited outside the door, but kept her focus on the women in the room—who, when they saw Belle, made room for her on the sofa.

No sooner had Belle accepted the proffered seat than her hair turned blonde, her bosom appeared larger, and she wore a bright red dress *cut down to there.*

A replica of Margaret—or—was it Margaret?

Ice clinked in highball glasses as the gathering women sipped, chatted, and laughed. A smoke cloud swirled over their heads and twined in and out of ornate hairdos as they puffed on cigarettes in long black holders.

How did they breathe without choking?

Belle looked to chat as casually as she might in a sorority full of millennial students. One of the women even offered Belle a puff on her cigarette, and Belle accepted.

Duh! Sidra pulled out her cell phone and snapped a picture, and with the snap, her phone went dead. She dumped it back in her pocket, uncertain if she captured anything.

How long she watched the dream—or the pit she'd fallen into, Sidra had no idea. Somewhere in the midst of the altered universe, she thought about the dogs but didn't dare take her eyes off of Belle and…and…the *women*?

The soft glow of daybreak startled Sid. She blinked and blinked again. The women inside were gone. Belle stood in the doorway facing Sidra, her glazed eyes as puzzled-looking as Sidra felt.

Jenkins barked, jumping up on Belle. Slider stood back watching.

"What the hell happened, Belle?"

"I—I don't know. Nothing happened, I guess. Did you see anything? It's okay, Jenkins. I'm okay." She rubbed Jenkins's red fur and then eased her paws down to the porch. "I went inside, but like you said, there wasn't anyone there… I turned around and came out. Why?" She looked at the sky, "And why is the sun rising at 2 a.m.?"

"It isn't two, Belle; it's closer to seven. You've been in there for hours. Don't you remember?"

"No, I haven't." She pulled out her cell phone and checked the clock—2:15 am. "Look! See, it says the time is two. I just went in and out."

Puzzled as to who was crazy and who wasn't, Sidra yanked hers out of her pocket, surprised she now had service. 7:05 am. She flipped it around to show Belle, who stared a second, then turned around and grabbed the doorknob. Locked—as usual.

"Oh my god, what just happened?" Belle wobbled. "What the *hell* happened, Sidra?"

"I don't know, but one thing for sure, my cell phone was dead, now it isn't."

Belle mumbled something about a scripture verse as Sidra took her arm, and the two hurried back to Fancy.

Inside, Sidra put on a fresh pot of coffee, toasted a couple of slices of bread while Belle sat on the sofa, eyes transfixed, skin pale.

Hot cups in hand, Sidra forced one on Belle and then went back for the toast. Seated, they nibbled on the toast while their thoughts settled—actually, their nerves— which jittered and jangled into Never, Never Land.

The dogs rested uneasily on the floor, their eyes coated in concern. Every now and then, Jenkins eased over, stole a sniff from Belle, then returned to her warm spot on the rug beside Slider—who looked as confused as Sidra felt.

Belle placed her empty cup on the table and stretched, taking in several deep breaths and releasing them slowly before she spoke. "So you're telling me, I stayed inside Miss Lilly for hours?"

"What I'm telling you is you went in at two—a little after, I guess—and the women didn't disappear like they did when I went in. Rather the two on the sofa moved over and made room for you in the middle, continuing their conversations and smokes like you belonged there."

Belle grabbed the neckline of her gray sweatshirt and sniffed. "I don't smell smoke."

"What about your skin?"

Belle sniffed her hand and coughed. "Smoke."

"What?"

"My hand smells like cigarette smoke, here, smell."

Sidra leaned over and sniffed. "Then, I'm not crazy. I thought at first I might be hallucinating."

Quiet. Total silence. Except for the dogs' heavy breathing and an occasional sniff.

"Okay. So you say you stood there and watched the whole thing?"

Sid nodded.

"For hours? You stood and watched until I came out? You didn't go anywhere?"

"Well, it didn't seem long—actually, it seemed like

you'd just gone inside when the sunrise startled me, and you came out."

"And they acted like they knew me—like I was one of them?"

"Well, actually, now that I think about it, they seemed to defer to you—in conversation, in offering cigarettes, in…"

"Defer?"

"All of you were laughing and talking like you shared funny stories, but I didn't hear a sound."

"And I looked the same, the whole time?"

Sidra thought back. "No…come to think about it…no. Soon as you sat down…you…your clothes sort of…melded…into theirs."

"Melded? What do you mean—like morphed?"

Sidra struggled for words to describe what she couldn't be sure she saw or how to make sense of any of it. "Well, umm…let me think…your hair…wasn't dark anymore."

"My hair changed colors? To what, pray tell?" The pitch of Belle's voice grew higher and the volume, louder.

"You had long blonde curls."

"Long blonde…?"

"That's not all, your clothes…it was like one of those virtual age progression images. Your clothes became a bright red dress cut down to here and sprinkled with gold-sequins."

"Jesus Christ Mary Magdalene."

The two sat in silence for what seemed forever.

However, Warren didn't stay quiet.

Okay, baby sister. You're getting the big picture now, finally. Have to draw the dang thing with crayons for you. You have to tell her, NOW. Don't make the poor girl piece all this together by herself. Help her. Tell her what I told you.

Alright alright, Warren, okay, if that's what it takes to get you to shut up.

"Remember, I told you about my brother, Warren? How he knew stuff most people didn't?"

Belle pulled her attention back to Sidra. "Yes, I remember, and I said you also had the gift."

"Yeah, well…there's something—"

"Just say it, Sidra."

"He confirmed Margaret, the woman in the painting at the store—"

"Yes? What about it?"

"—is your mother's ancestor."

Three gold sequins, seemingly from nowhere, appeared in Belle's lap.

Chapter Seventeen
Miss Fancy

Caught inside this vortex, not of our making, we sisters shelter for protection, not only from the piercing arrows of judgment, of ridicule and hatred shot at us from those without a clue what we lived—live—through, and even those not always of this earth, but a vortex nonetheless.

We circle around past, present, and future generations of women. For dignity and honor. For worthy self-image, fairness and respect for the marvel of co-creation. For birth and rebirth. For all those things we never experienced—all because of *him*.

When those women arrived a few days ago, we whispered amongst ourselves not to worry, no one stays long. They won't either. Not when they get a glimpse of the way things *really* are. Things no rational mind believes.

When flesh and blood and beating hearts plunge into a world where absolutely nothing fits. Where everything threatens their safe, predictable world, they hasten back into their comfortable nests, unwilling to challenge a world not of their making.

Perhaps we come across too strong, perhaps we frighten, yet it is not our intent. We do, however resent the pointing and the snickering when they speak of our past. Are they not left with the taste of gall after spewing foul words from the cesspool deep within? Don't they realize we hear their words and feel their barbs?

We expect to once again be ignored, denied existence, denied understanding, acceptance, and justice—left to remain victims ourselves. We do what we must to survive in a patriarchal world full of those who fear our power—our creative abilities, our gentleness—our strength.

Still we seek escape—like a raindrop seeks the ocean.

Regardless of how long we seek such, we remain unable to do so.

Why, you ask?

The sins of our father trap us, a father who escaped accountability in this life and left us to pay his price.

True, we are not proud of everything we did. Anger and revenge bring out the shadow side of our nature—and indeed, we had reason to be angry—wounded by our father, left to feel unworthy, without clue of who we were—the power and the beauty available to us had we only known. Maybe if we had, then forgiveness might have come. Instead, we did what we needed to do to survive while in physical form—laid ourselves on the sacrificial altar.

We suffered—immeasurably—and still do.

Yet these two, the white-haired woman, something about her crosses both worlds—definitely an intuitive. Perhaps she can help us—that is if we can tap into her love of *travel.*

The young one, she fits right in. One might guess

she'd fallen backward through time. People talk about time travel, but they don't know the half of it. Some might go backward or forward, but not us. We sit stuck for eternity—condemned by events out of our control, innocent bystanders watching the devil run his course until someone's wisdom and determination leads to our release.

We—my sisters and I—often wonder what all happened to Mother. Last thing we saw, he'd wrapped his huge, grotesque looking paws around her hair, shoved her up into the buggy, and climbed in behind her. While screams able to curdle blood ripped through Mother as she cried out our names, his angry whip snapped and slashed at the horses until only the swirling dust gave hint of his escape.

Yet we saw her, albeit from the other side, burning in the house fire that night. Did she somehow escape before he got out of town, or did he shove her out of the carriage at the last minute?

Save his own hide, did he? What about ours? What about all those tortured souls he left behind and even those who came after? What about those used and abused behind these walls? Where were they, and what traps us here, unable to escape?

After the goings on last night, I figured those two would be gone by daylight—like the newlywed couple on their wedding night. Those two were so much in love, I felt certain they'd understand our cry for help.

So much for that idea.

If these two aren't gone by nightfall, I'll pay another visit—but this time, I'll try another tactic.

Chapter Eighteen

After breakfast, Sidra lingered at the table sipping a second cup of coffee while still trying to wrap her head around what happened earlier that morning before and until daybreak.

"Tell me again what you saw, Sid," Belle asked. "I have no recollection of anything except smelling like cigarette smoke. I wished you'd thought to—"

"Take a picture," Sidra cried out at the resurrected memory. "I did, I did. I forgot I did right before my cell went dead." She leapt from the table and snatched her phone off the charger. "Gallery, Photos," she thumbed through the images. "Yes, here it is, look." She rammed the phone towards Belle.

"I don't see anything—other than those you took driving up. Where is it?"

"Right there, the last one," she took the phone, found the photo again, and pointed.

Belle shook her head. "Same photo."

"What?"

Sidra scrolled down and found it again. "I don't understand; why can't you see it?" As she watched, the photo slowly faded—evaporated.

Shaken, they spent the remainder of the day sightseeing, hoping to get their minds off of what they'd seen, not seen—and smelled.

Darkness came, and Sidra used it as an excuse to escape to her room. Perplexed by everything that had transpired, Sidra wanted nothing more than to retire early. Belle followed suit.

Sidra felt like if she didn't get time to think, she'd go crazy. Confusion and concern consumed her. What had she missed? Why did the photo on her phone simply disappear? What weird world—twilight zone—had they entered? She crawled in bed, with Slider right behind her.

Hoping to reassure herself, or confirm her suspicion she'd gone crazy, she clicked on the photo gallery once again. She'd taken the damn picture. She knew she had. She'd seen it. Or had she gone slap dab crazy?

She scanned the last photos she'd taken, and there wasn't a single picture of Miss Scarlet from the evening before. Certain she remembered correctly, that her phone went dead after the first snap, she replayed the whole thing in her head then went to her photo gallery.

Again, she saw photos taken earlier, but not the one she snapped the night before. Was she losing her mind? Had she lost it?

She looked again.

"Okay, what am I missing?" She had seen the women, Belle went in, talked with them, Sid took the photo, and saw it before her phone went dead.

Chapter Nineteen

Sidra held onto the information about the photo, and the next day suggested they visit the local historical society. Couldn't hurt—might help. Hopefully, there were records about the houses.

The volunteers shared what little information they had of the houses—otherwise known as The Three Sisters. Over the years, different people lived there. None seemed to stay very long. Originally, a larger house sat on the now vacant lot next door and burned, years later. No evidence existed of who owned them, who leased them, how long they'd stayed.

They saw an ancient photo of the houses before any other business developed. In the photo, shot from below, three narrow white houses stood over the town, almost like sentries—all by themselves. Sidra tried to find the date the photo was taken, but it had not been recorded.

Discouraged, Sidra and Belle thanked the volunteer and were walking to their vehicle when a man they'd seen inside strolled up.

"I heard you asking about the three sisters up on the hill. I know a little about them, if you'd like to hear."

"Of course. We'd love to." Excitement flavored Belle's voice.

"Mind if I smoke?" he asked.

"Sure, go ahead."

The tall, thin man pulled a cigarette out of his shirt pocket, lit it, and took a puff.

He squinted from the smoke curling around his face. "All I know is those houses are said to be haunted. Over the years, different people have lived in them or had businesses in the houses, but none stayed long. I remember a beauty shop once, and later a tattoo parlor. Last one was one of them Bed & Breakfast outfits. That business didn't last through their first customers. These young newlyweds booked one of the rooms for their honeymoon. You know, old Victorian home, newly refurbished and all, and in a tourist town to boot."

"Sounds like a neat place to stay," Belle said.

"Well, it didn't quite turn out like they expected. Story goes, in the middle of the first night, a ghost showed up sitting on their bed. Scared the bee gee out of 'em. They snatched their things and hightailed it out town, never to be seen or heard from again."

They chatted with the man a little longer, thanking him for the information, and he went on his way.

Once in the car Belle said, "You know, I find it very strange. Something is missing."

"We're overlooking details—for sure." By the time Sidra turned into the driveway and parked, the sky opened up a deluge of rain. Both made a run for it but got soaked anyway. The dogs, huddled together under the porch, scampered up to join them inside.

Dogs dried, Sid and Belle changed into dry clothes and prepared a supper—neither of them much interested in food.

"Well, I guess this means we have a good excuse to not visit the houses tonight." Belle looked relieved when saying the words.

Sidra laughed. "Well, I'm with you, kid. I say let's take a break, get a good night's sleep, and see where we are tomorrow."

No sooner had the two agreed than they heard footsteps running up on the porch and a knock on the door. Belle peaked through the window. "Damn, it's Sawyer. I thought he'd left town."

He knocked a second time.

"You want to let him in, or keep him outside in the rain?" Sidra laughed at her own joke—or was it?

Belle opened the door. There stood what looked like a drowned rat. "I thought you'd left town? What are you doing here? I told you—

"Just hear me out, Belle. Hear me out."

Sidra brought him a dry towel. "Might as well stop dripping all over the hardwood."

"Thanks." He grabbed the terry cloth, wiped his face, and dried off his clothes. "Belle, I just… I can't leave just yet. Maxx called and said—"

"Said what? What in the world could Maxx say that might prevent you from going back to your job—your precious church." Derision coated the last few words.

"I—he, to tell you the truth, I'm not sure either. I just told him you wouldn't leave until you figured out this mess. And he advised me to stay. Said you'd need me when you learned the truth."

Belle choked. Sidra came close. Belle recovered, eyes wide, hands on her hips. "What, pray tell, does Maxx know that he isn't telling me? What? He swore to me he didn't know why my mother kept these houses, but he must. That pisses the hell out of me."

"No need to use bad language, Belle—"

"And don't you tell me how to talk. I'm a grown woman. I can say anything I damn well please. If you don't like it, there's the door."

Sidra looked away, knowing sacred territory surfaced. Belle's right to claim her own strength, her own voice, not controlled by her father, in whatever guise—even if his words and attitude came out of Sawyer's mouth.

"He's channeling through you, Sawyer. Don't you see it? He's always channeled himself through your voice. He's made you his puppet. Think for yourself, damn it."

The gates of hell opened. The storm outside grew more furious, slamming against the windows, branches scratching to get inside, eager, deadly. Startled by the intensity, fearing the windows or the roof might fly off any minute, Sidra glanced from Sawyer to Belle and back again.

Sawyer's beet-red face glowed in the darkening room, his hands pulled into tight fists. Then, as quickly, he let out a long sigh. "Belle, believe it or not, I am on your side. You can choose to believe me or not, but I am. I always have been."

The thought of a deal with the devil shivered through Sidra. Was Sawyer really on Belle's side, or his own, or the reincarnate of Belle's father or mother? Right now, none of this made any sense. Belle warred between opposing forces. Herself, and her love for her family— which may or not have been as perfect as they pretended. Or did they? Did they pretend, or were they on some kind of mission to—to what?

Oh good lord, Warren—where are you now? You got me into this mess, and I am in over my head.

Were Belle on a mission for the dark side, surely Sidra would have known that, felt that. Or would she? Sawyer? Was he the good guy? Was Belle's father truly as holy as he pretended? What about her mother?

By the time Sidra processed all the questions in her

head, she saw Sawyer standing alone, holding a pillow and blanket. Belle wasn't in the room.

"Where's Belle?" Sidra looked around the room. No Belle, and no Jenkins—not even Slider. "Did she give you the bedcovers? Why?"

Sawyer nodded and dumped the covers on the small love seat. "The storm's growing worse. You must not have heard me ask if I could bunk here till morning. He glanced behind him at the sofa, the very small sofa for a six-foot man.

Outside, thunder and lightning raged. Inside, the house went dark.

"Wow. Got any candles? I can light them for you."

"No need," Sidra said, feeling her way through the kitchen to the small staircase and felt her way upstairs with a great amount of dis-ease—not over the darkness— but the presence of Sawyer in the house all night. What she needed more than anything was a good night's sleep. Between the storms—the one outside, the one inside, and the one raging inside her soul, she doubted sleep showed.

Shivering, she felt her way across the room and found Slider, dried off and snoozing atop the covers on her bed. After peeling off her still-damp clothes, she scratched around until she found her housecoat, slipped into it, and eased under the covers. She fell into a deep sleep and dreamed of a raging river overflowing its banks and pulling her into it, dragging her down, down, down. No breath, she couldn't breathe in the depths. She knew she must surface to get air…she wasn't really in the water, a riptide of a dream pulled her…why couldn't she awake…must… get…out… She tugged and fought to drive away the fog, sat straight up in bed, and looked for comfort from Slider.

He stood straight up in bed, hair raised, riveted to the figure dressed in a yellow gauze clothing, sitting on the foot of Sid's bed, crying as though heartbroken.

"Mother, mother, where are you? How could you

have let him do that? Bad enough to others, but to us, his own daughters?"

Chills washed over Sidra. She pulled her robe tighter and tried not to breathe, afraid the figure would disappear, and at the same time, afraid it wouldn't.

The young woman continued sobbing and repeating the same sentence over and over.

Sidra wondered whether or not she still dreamed, or whether the figure was a figment of her imagination, which grew more vivid every day. Hopefully, she was going crazy. If not, she had idea what to do, or when the figure would leave. If she left, where would she go, and why had this figure had shown up on Sid's bed, and not Belle's? Or maybe she had. Maybe—could a ghost appear in two places at once?

She looked over at Slider. He still hadn't moved a muscle. He stared at Sidra like he wanted to say *what in the hell is this? Do something.*

Then, Slider's hackles lowered, and he crawled to the figure and rested his head in her lap. As he did, the figure's hand rested on Slider and rubbed his head gently. Like the two knew each other.

Now, what did she do?

Warren, where are you? Why aren't you here helping me make sense of all of this?

Then she knew why not. Because he trusted her to figure it out, to get there by herself. He trusted her ability, else he would not have willed her his precious Third Eye Intuitive Investigations. As though leaving her his detective agency weren't enough, his specialty, and now hers, was conducting intuitive investigation. He kept telling her she had *the gift* but…

"Lilly? Are you Miss Lilly?" Sid stammered the question to the apparition at the foot of her bed.

The moaning stopped.

So did Sidra's heart. At least it felt like it stopped. Or maybe her lungs were frozen solid.

I begged her to stop him, early on, I begged. Perhaps she tried, I know she tried, but that only brought his wrath down on her. The last thing I heard was a fist slamming her to the ground.

Warren? Is that you?

Silence.

Okay, not Warren, but words from somewhere flooded her, then stopped, along with the specter at the foot of her bed.

Slider glanced back over his shoulder at Sidra, let out the thinnest of whines, then crept over and rested his head in her lap.

"You saw it too, didn't you, sweetheart?"

A sudden movement across the room startled Sidra. She clutched Slider tight, until Jenkins barged around her bedroom door, darted across the room, and landed atop the two of them.

"Oh boy, are we the only ones going crazy? Or perhaps, we are the sane ones, guys. However, if we are the sane ones, what do we do now?" She whispered, uncertain if she should wake Belle, when a squeak sounded on the stairs. Terrified, close to petrified, she struck a match and, with trembling hands, lit the candle beside her bed.

The wick flared just in time to reveal Sawyer in her now-open doorway. Nagging fear and more than a little distrust wriggled its way inside her chest. Sidra pulled the dogs closer. "You have no right coming in here. Get out," she hissed.

Chapter Twenty

Sawyer shoved his palms out towards her. "Shhh, shhh. It's okay; it's okay. I heard something and thought I better check on you two. Is everything okay? Where's Belle?"

"In her room, I guess; I haven't—"

"Hold on; let me check."

Barely able to discern his figure in the dim light, Sidra watched him cross the parlor, Jenkins, hot on his heels. She tiptoed over to see him peak around the doorway of Belle's bedroom, then come back her way, but without Jenkins.

"She's okay," he whispered. "Sound asleep. Jenkins curled up beside her. I feared Jenkins might argue me checking on Belle; instead, she only gave me one last warning look and settled down beside her. What's going on?"

Although unsure if his presence offered relief or

more fear, she sucked in a breath and admitted, "I…we…thought we saw something, it's nothing."

"Your hands are shaking, Ms. Smart. I don't mean to be intrusive, but…"

She hadn't seen this side of Sawyer. Was he trying to suck her in? Could she trust him? Be honest? Good grief, a fifty-year-old woman, well, maybe a few years older, and she still questioned her judgment.

It's all your fault, Warren. You got me into this, then deserted me—actually, deserted me before I even knew where I headed.

"I get your hesitancy, Mrs. Smart—

"Ms."

"Excuse me?"

"It's Ms. Smart—not Mrs."

"Ms. Smart. I know you aren't sure you can trust me. I get that. Hell, Belle doesn't trust me."

His use of the unexpected four-letter word told Sidra she, and maybe Belle, didn't really know this man. Or maybe they did, and this was his attempt to cause doubt.

Maybe.

"I understand why she might, why you might. I've worked hard to model myself after her father. Studied his words, his manner of speaking, of writing, read everything he put in my hands." Sawyer sat, rather, collapsed, on the edge of the bed near Slider, who jumped at first, then eased over, sniffed the man, and scooted closer, like he met him for the first time. Perhaps he had, at least the real Sawyer.

Or should she believe this man beside her? Was he deceptive? Trying to be? Or…

"I…love… Belle," he stuttered.

Something about the pauses between his words made Sid question whether she should believe him. Her first impression had been that he kept a tight lid on his true self, perhaps not only from others but also from himself. She learned a long time ago to never trust anyone with all the answers, about life, relationships, or God.

Uneasy with Sawyer sitting on her bed in the middle of the night, even though the electricity had come back on, Sidra threw back the blankets and stood. "Want to go downstairs and put on a pot of coffee? I bought hazelnut flavor the other day. I've been wanting to try it." Straightening her housecoat, she slid her feet into fuzzy slippers.

Unshaven, disheveled, and looking dazed, he appeared to have traveled a million miles from where he sat. Slider looked from him to Sidra as though asking, *are we going or not? Let me know because I'm not missing a moment of this conversation.*

"Sawyer?"

He shuddered back to the present. "Yeah, yeah, I'd like that. He rose and motioned Sidra to go first. She did, with Slider at her heels.

After the coffee brewed, they gathered their mugs and sat around the kitchen table, Slider at her feet.

"What's going on, Sawyer? What is it that you're not saying? I daresay you have never said it. Your confession a couple of minutes ago blew my mind. I'm sure it is going to blow Belle's. Maybe that's why she doesn't like you. She's smart, and if you've been inauthentic with her, she would know it. You sure didn't do yourself any favors copying her father's ways. They repulsed her."

He stared at her for the longest, then and gave a long, loud sigh. "What a breath of honesty and frankness. I'm not accustomed to that. However, you nailed it. I got into it for the wrong reasons and before I knew it…"

"Why did you?"

"I knew if I didn't, I could never expect to minister to people. I so admired him…well, at first I did, then by the time I got deeper into it and learned… I didn't know how to get out. Belle said she didn't see me at the cemetery, wondered why I wasn't there beside her. I told her I couldn't get to her because of the crowd, but the truth is, I didn't go."

"So you lied."

He ducked his chin to his chest. "I've lied for so long, I've gotten used to the guilt."

"Why did you not go—and why lie about it?"

"I didn't go because, because… I don't really know why I didn't go. I dressed for it, shaved, put on my best preacher-suit and tie, got in my spotlessly clean car, and headed that way. But the closer I got, the more I knew I had no tears for the man. Yes, he treated me nice, although superior—always superior—but… I don't know; it's like a floodgate of lies I'd lived broke through the dam. I just…"

"What are you not saying, Sawyer. I need something else. I need you to say what you want to say, but have never been brave enough to say."

"I don't know if I can. You know, after a while you believe your own lies."

"Who else have you lied to?

"Implicit or explicit?"

"Both, I guess."

He paused, head sinking deeper, shoulders closing in around him. "How about everyone in the world—the whole fucking world!"

He grew silent. Sidra waited.

"It isn't easy…"

Sidra didn't say a word. She simply sat in silence, giving him time to release a lifetime of grief.

After he settled down, she continued her silence, intending not to break it, but then words came without her permission. "You love, Belle…but…"

"I've tried to love her like a lover…but…"

"You love her like?"

"A sister."

"Why is that?"

The time between the silence grew larger, longer, until sleet filled in the spaces with pings against the windowpane near them. The sky had lightened, and Sidra glanced outside to see snow now mixed in with the sleet.

Sawyer didn't seem to notice.

"Okay, here it is… I loved her father more than I loved her.

"Why is that?" She nudged for full authenticity and self-awareness.

"Because…"

"Say it, Sawyer. It is important to say whatever the word is you most don't want to say.

"I'm not gay, but my feelings towards him were different—like none I'd ever experienced before."

"Did he return your love?"

"Not really. More than anything, I felt like my adoration of him fed his ego. I do know this, however, not only was he not gay, but he was *very* heterosexual. I know. I witnessed several female church members enter his office and leave in disarray. I always expected one of them to come forward, to let others know…but he held some kind of magical power over them. They worshipped him."

"Like you did."

"Like I did, yes."

"And you've never admitted this to anyone, or figured out why you felt the way you did?"

Sawyer shook his head, and the tears started again.

Sidra moved across the kitchen to refill their coffee cups, feeling a need to give Sawyer a little time and space to collect himself. While she poured the coffee, she noticed ten red-painted toenails just at the edge of the small curved stairwell.

Belle. Now she knew too. Sidra considered calling her down but decided against it. Instead, she resumed her seat at the table. "It's okay, Sawyer. Your secret is safe with me.

"However, I know you still have a job at the church you might need to keep, at least for a while, but you might consider being honest with Belle."

"I want to tell Belle, I must."

"You already did," Belle scooted down around the curved stairwell, gathered her wrapper closed, and stepped into the tiny kitchen. "Your voices woke me. I started down to the kitchen, but then… Sorry, I didn't mean to eavesdrop, I—"

"Belle? Sorry for you to learn this way, but…"

Belle's countenance softened, she rested her hand on Sawyer's shoulder and soon accepted the proffered coffee from Sidra.

"Learn what? That you didn't love me?" Belle chuffed. The news was not news at all, but a long-known fact. One she'd known forever and the very reason why she rejected every attempt her father made to connect them.

"You…knew?" Sawyer stuttered.

"One thing you haven't learned about me, Sawyer, is I'm smarter than my father."

He stared at his wringing hands, now in his lap. "I guess, I guess…"

"You thought he knew everything, and everything he knew was gospel. Is that it?"

"No…not really. To tell you the truth, I don't know what I believed. I just hung to his coattail…like…like it offered normalcy."

"What aren't you telling us, Sawyer?" Belle pushed.

He hesitated then said, "I suppose the foundation is… You see… I'm a bastard. I never knew my father. My mother, well, let's just say she didn't do the best she could. I was born in a prison infirmary. Evidently, my father was an inmate as well, but they sure didn't have conjugal visits then. How she got with an inmate… Well, I don't have a clue."

"Maybe it wasn't an inmate. Don't they have male guards sometimes?"

"This one did. I suppose it could have been a guard, or who knows, maybe the warden. Or maybe I'm the byproduct of the Immaculate Conception."

"So, why me?" Belle leaned in closer to hear Sawyer's words, which were now barely above a whisper.

"Safety. Security. I thought if I tried hard enough, lived righteously enough, I'd burn away the sins of my mother and father. Your father offered me that."

"Did he know your past?"

"I don't know; we never talked about it, but…"

"What?"

"I always wondered why he sought me out…found me on the streets of Houston, fighting for food, fighting off gang rapes, and everything else life offers those occupants of nowhere."

"When was this?" Sidra scooted her chair closer connecting the tiny pieces of information much like the street outside collected sheets of ice.

"I was a young teenager. He found me one day, begging for quarters on the street corner when he stopped at the light."

Belle looked as enthralled by the story as Sidra felt. Where was he heading, and did any of this come close to the truth?

Sidra put several eggs on to boil, patted canned biscuits onto a cookie sheet, and shoved them in the oven, all while keeping tuned into the conversation at the table. Something told her there was much more behind this whole thing, but wanted to allow Belle and Sawyer time to open up with each other.

"What happened after that?" Belle asked.

"He invited me to get in the car."

"Oh God, I fear what you're going to say next."

"It isn't what you're thinking. He didn't take advantage of me."

"You mean no sex?"

"Not at all. Actually, he took me to a restaurant, bought us both a meal, and asked me to share my story. I told him I'd lived in foster homes until I ran away, fed up with all the bullshit, people acting like they cared about you, when all they really wanted was the few dollars offered by the state."

"Did he learn about your parents?"

Sawyer nodded. "What little I knew. Belle, he showed me the most compassion I'd ever known."

"Why?"

"I don't know. At the time it didn't matter. But something tells me he knew more than he ever admitted."

"About your past, you mean?"

"Yes, because once I overheard your parents fighting over me and something about Arkansas. About some property or something like that—I assume these houses. He kept saying she should sell them before the truth got out, and it ruined his career. How she'd never have all the nice things she loved."

"Really? That sounds like him. He always used my mom's love of nice things to control her."

Sidra prepared hot biscuits, eggs, and jelly and brought them each a plate of food.

"I don't mean to interrupt this conversation, but we all look like a little physical nourishment could help us deal with what we still face. Whatever that is. I'm not sure any of us are ready."

They accepted the plates of food and ate, but continued the discussion.

"When I learned you were coming to Arkansas something clicked inside me. I knew, I knew, Belle, somehow I was connected to it."

"Is your name really Sawyer?" Belle asked.

"I…no…it isn't. Your father helped me change it. He said that was the best way to start all over again."

"Wow. When was this?"

"Oh, I guess ten years ago? Before he enrolled me in the seminary. He had connections, and I was able to get in without a high school diploma or a college degree." He shook his head and laughed. "That man had connections…and power. I owed him. I owe him. That's why I stood by him, even when I disagreed with a lot of the things he said and did. He owned me, Belle, but as far as I know, everything he did for me was in my best interest."

Don't buy that, Sidra.

Okay, so you're still here, sweet brother. Somehow, I am not surprised.

Belle cleared her throat and sat straighter. "Well, you think you knew my father…and indeed you do know more about him in areas that I don't, but I also know he never did anything that wasn't in his best interest."

"Maybe. All I know is my experience with him."

Sidra collected the empty dishes and washed them. While she did, both Belle and Sawyer sat in dead silence. Their breathing sounded heavy, deep, their lungs forced to function.

Outside, snow piled higher on the window ledge. For good or bad, it looked like they were snowed in for the day with lots of time to talk. Where the conversation might take them, she hadn't a clue.

What she did know was that they were on the road to truth.

"Sawyer, do you remember anything at all about your mother or father?" Sidra asked, replenishing their coffee mugs.

"Barely, barely. I see a woman in my mind, I guess it was my mother…not sure…she… I seemed to be a bother to her. But she fed and dressed me as long as they let me stay with her. Then the guards came, and I don't remember ever seeing her again. Next thing I see is riding in a car and getting out at a strange house. A woman came out, snatched me from the arms of whoever held me. After that, it was a long list of one home, one family after another. I see a familiar-looking man pop into my memory from time to time… I've always wondered who he was, but… I can't get a clear enough picture of him to know who it might have been.

"The foster homes grew increasing miserable—no one mistreated me, but I just always felt like a zygote dropped out of the wrong basket. Never fit. I ran away, far away, so no one would ever find me. Escaped to the big city where it's easy for boys to get lost. No one cared about them. Not even sure how long that lasted, but, then, one day this nice guy drove by. He acted like he knew me, but I knew he didn't. Had no idea at that point, he was a preacher." Sawyer clasped Belle's hands and squeezed.

She let him.

"My father."

"Yes, your father."

"He provided for me, found a boarding school, and paid for my tuition for several years—until I had enough of that and ran away again.

"Then once again, one day, he pulled his car alongside me on the street. He looked familiar. I guess that's why I went with him. Only later did he remind me who he was and that he'd been searching for me for a couple of years. The boarding school had notified him I left. Said he scoured the dark back alleys of Houston several times, hoping he'd see me."

"Why?"

"Not real sure. Yes, the man was known for his big heart, but I always felt like something else drove him."

"I can assure you there was. Like I said before, I never knew my father to do anything that didn't benefit him and his carefully constructed persona."

Sidra flinched. In a way, she understood Belle's feelings, based on her own experience. Sidra had to admit she'd lived with that in her own marriage, which is what contributed to the divorce.

However, perhaps there was more to Belle's dad than she knew.

And to Sam.

Maybe.

Chapter Twenty-One

Sidra inhaled a deep breath, held it, and then exhaled. The tension felt like melted butter sliding down her neck and shoulders.

"I don't know about you two," she said, "but I am in serious need of a shower and clean clothes. I'm beginning to smell rank."

Not to mention time to think, to order her thoughts. Before they left Texas, the job had seemed simple. It didn't now—and she hadn't a clue what to do next.

She headed upstairs to the shower.

"Who wants to go next?" Sidra bounded downstairs refreshed and clear-headed. Belle pointed to Sawyer.

"Men first."

He gave a chuckle. "Don't believe that old stereotype about men dressing faster than women."

"We'll take our chances," Sid and Belle both said, laughing.

"Okay, don't say you weren't warned," he called as he headed upstairs, humor in his voice.

Sure enough, Sawyer's ablutions lasted longer than Belle's and Sid's combined, but when he and Belle both finished, he suggested they move upstairs. "You know, it's a lot warmer there after all the hot showers. We haven't lost power yet, but I think it would be wise to save the dried wood as our emergency stash. Once ice-coated tree branches start falling that's all it takes to plunge us into darkness and without heat."

They collected a few candles, a box of matches, the flashlight, and followed the rising warmer air to the sitting room upstairs.

Belle and Sid curled up on either end of the sofa and tucked their feet up under a mutual blanket. Meanwhile, Sawyer paced the floor, peered out at the weather, and perched on the arm of a side chair in the corner.

"Okay, where were we?"

Reluctant to revisit her night caller, Sidra swallowed hard and cut her hooded gaze to Sawyer. "Belle, I haven't had a chance to tell you what happened last night. Actually early this morning."

"What?" Belle looked surprised. "You didn't go back to the houses, did you?"

"No, not in this weather, but—"

"What?"

"Well, one of them—I guess it was one of them— came over to this house."

"I don't believe this!" Belle's hand snatched Sidra's blanketed feet and squeezed.

The room fell silent.

"Well, hell yes," Belle said. "I guess right now, there

is nothing I can't believe. Tell me."

"I don't know how long I'd slept, but it seemed like hours, when this loud sobbing roused me. Like a bolt, I sat up, heart pounding, adrenaline raging. A sliver of moonlight streamed through the window and illuminated what looked like a shadowy figure sitting on the foot of my bed sobbing, arguing with someone—maybe her mother, I guess. The entity kept asking why she and her sisters were abandoned. She kept mentioning a he or him. I assume she referred to her father."

"Who was the woman? Could you tell? Guess?" Belle's grip tightened.

"I assume it was Fancy—she wore this long yellow gauze dress." As she spoke, Sidra eased her foot from Belle's vise-like grip.

"The same color as this house—or close to it. I wondered why she chose my bedroom. Slider saw her, too, stood straight up in bed, hackles raised…then…"

"Then what?"

"Then, Sawyer came in. He saw her too, because we looked at each other, questioning the other's sanity—at least I questioned mine. Sawyer?"

"Well, I don't believe in ghosts, but if I did, it sure looked like what I'd expect."

He went on to say he heard the crying from downstairs, thought it came from Sidra's bedroom, and came to check. His presence seemed to startle the entity, and she disappeared. "That's why we were downstairs having coffee before the sun came up."

Stunned, Belle looked from Sidra to Sidra's bedroom and back again, clueless, it seemed, as what to do next. Sidra understood that feeling, for it matched hers to a T.

Without another word, the three gathered the candles and moved back downstairs. Whether to get as far away from last night's entity or not, Sidra didn't know, but she did not object.

As though by some unspoken agreement, no one said

another word about the situation they did not understand and, truth be told, were not sure they wanted to understand.

Ignore became the operative word of the afternoon. Small talk moved from penny bets on the depth of the snowfall, to when it might stop, to the idea of making snow ice cream. Sawyer drew the short straw simply by being the minority. He grabbed a big plastic bowl and serving spoon, darted outside, and collected the main ingredient while Sidra gathered sugar and milk.

The unexpected loud, insistent ringing of Belle's cell phone brought the activities to a halt. She yanked the phone out of her pocket and glanced at the caller ID. "It's Maxx. What in the world?" She punched the answer button.

"Maxx, what's going on?"

Pause

"Oh, Sawyer is here with us. I didn't know he hadn't let anyone know where he was."

Pause.

"Someone's looking for him? They called you? Why? Okay. Who was it, what did they want?"

After a few more minutes, she punched off the phone.

"What's going on?" Sawyer looked clueless.

"You didn't notify your employer you were leaving town?"

"I certainly did. Let the Chairman of Deacons know—actually, he encouraged me to come check on you. Said a lot of church members were worried about your welfare. What else did Maxx say?"

"Said some man came looking for you—said he used to know your mother, but heard you had changed your name."

Sawyer walked to the window and peered outside.

Pay attention, here, Sid, something's going on—pieces of the puzzle are coming together. I feel it in my bones—well, metaphorically speaking.

Sidra walked to Sawyer and rested her hand on his

shoulder. "What is it, Sawyer? What's happening? Got a clue who this guy is?"

He shook his head, looking confused.

"Okay, don't worry. We will piece this together. Just hang on. Somehow you must be tied to this whole mystery more than you know. We will untangle the threads, piece by piece."

Belle's cell phone rang again—startling them out of the million miles they'd traveled since the earlier call.

"It's Maxx again." She punched it on. "Maxx? What the hell's going on?" She listened silently, punched off the connection, and sat in stunned silence.

"What is it," Sidra asked from across the room.

"He said never mind the earlier call. He'd just opened today's *Houston Chronicle* and noticed an article about a suspected murder last night. Seems witnesses describe what looked to be an intentional hit and run. The paper carried a photo of the victim—get this—the photo was the same man who came looking for Sawyer."

She glanced at Sawyer, as did Sidra. Confusion covered his face.

"Come sit, Sawyer." Sidra patted the chair beside her.

He flopped down, his arms dangling between his knees.

"Holy bejesus," he said. "I have no clue…"

Should she believe him? Sidra excused herself, ran upstairs to the bathroom, and stared at her reflection in the mirror. What was going on? What connection did Sawyer have with all this? Who the hell was looking for him, and why? She felt like a ball and chain tugged her toward a bottomless pit.

Warren, where are you? Why aren't you here now, when I need more information?

Because you have the information, little sister, all the threads, now just follow them. It's all there waiting for you.

"What the hell does that mean," she cried at her

mirrored reflection. "I have these houses, these specters, these people looking for answers and those who spent their lifetime trying to hide—something."

This word now, Sidra. This word now.

What word? What one word binds all the threads together? The houses? Fancy? Fancy, who sat on my bed last night crying, questioning her mother, why she left? Left her girls, women by that time evidently, they each had their own houses.

The women they saw at Miss Scarlet's—had Miss Fancy been one of them? What about Miss Lilly?

The very walls seem to cry out in pain.

The women are the connections…connections…connections.

She had to leave these two and do some digging on her own. Soon as the snow melted, she'd make some excuse and go investigating alone.

Intuitive Investigation, dear sister, remember?

Yes, dear brother. I remember.

Did Maxx give the name of the guy? That's the first thing. She could even go online and check the Houston newspapers. It should have the article. She returned to her bedroom.

What had she missed the night before?

Humbled, doubting her ability to figure out this confused mess, she flopped onto her bed, wishing she could talk to her mentor, George Leger, Annie, Ben, anyone?

You always have me, baby sister.

You told me I have all the threads, and I don't know what the hell that means, Warren, or what I have, so don't you come telling me that.

This word now—basement.

Basement? Well, if there were one, the door down to it would be covered in snow at the moment.

Unless there happened to be an inside door.

Inside? Where? Maybe in the small laundry area…

The broom closet, I'll check that first. Something odd behind the brooms and mops. I noticed it the first time I looked inside, but shrugged it off as just another weird feature of architecturally weird houses.

Deep in conversation with a dead man, the sounds of the other two coming up the stairs startled Sidra.

They rounded the stairwell, both shivering. "We decided to come back up here where it's warmer," Belle said. "Hope we're not disturbing you."

"Not at all, come on up. I'm thinking hot tea sounds good. You two thaw out. I'll run downstairs and put on the teakettle."

Soon as she opened the small, almost hidden door in the broom closet, odd odors slammed her in the face. Not single odors, but odors conglomerate—combined, melded into one horrific, stale, stagnant smell. Black. Black, dark, dank, and…

She stepped onto the landing, thankful to see a string dangling from a light bulb. She pulled it. Dust-filled cobwebs crisscrossed the stairs, and below that, pitch black. She felt and grabbed a broom to knock down enough webs to create a path through them. Her first step down—or was it her last—made the rotted stairs creak, moan, and shake.

It wasn't a full height basement, she had to stoop to move through, and it grew lower the further it went towards Miss Scarlet.

See, dear sister. Never ignore these intuitive feelings. They don't always add up to something that makes sense, but the broom closet sure did. No matter. Whatever's here has

likely been here a long time.

She pulled her jacket tighter and headed to a shelf full of old crates. She dug through tools and junk leftover from bygone eras, and found nothing that might connect with one of Warren's *threads*.

Half of an old, splintered door leaned against the back-dirt wall. Her hands felt like icicles. She wished for her gloves, but curiosity warmed them enough to shift the half door.

The dirt wall, a force within its own right, pulled her gaze downwards.

Three bone-white fingers protruded from the hardened mud.

Chapter Twenty-Two

Sidra stared—and kept staring. Were those bones? Human bones? If so, whose? Were they alone, or if she dug, would she find them connected to a hand, an arm, a torso? Should she tell the others first, or call the police?

Certain the basement was not acceptable as a burial ground, she dialed the authorities, and filed a report. Told the sergeant who she was, the address, and what she only now discovered in the basement.

"Excuse me, ma'am? You're who? Where are you, and you found what?"

"Sidra Smart, private detective from Texas. I'm here with a client. We are staying on the property my client recently inherited from her parents. I discovered a basement underneath the yellow house and went exploring. Found what looks like human remains—finger bones. I haven't started digging yet. Figured you might want to take a look before I do. Pretty sure this basement is not an approved burial ground—that is unless the house sits on some kind of sacred land of Native Americans."

"Excuse me—what address did you say?"

"Court Street, the three, century-old-houses on Court Street. Bright painted, gingerbread trim—"

"Got it. Know them. Hold on a minute."

She waited.

"Ms. Smart? Ma'am?" The sergeant came back online. "Please don't touch a thing. We will be there as soon as we can. This snowstorm might delay us, but please wait. Don't—"

"Don't touch a thing, I know. I won't. And we aren't going anywhere. We will be here."

She clicked off the call and wandered around, stepping around piles of junk, looking over her shoulder every now and then to make sure the finger bones indeed stayed where she found them. Still a little unsure whether they were a figment of her imagination or planted there by her dear departed brother. Since he planted the word *basement*, perhaps he planted the bones.

Intending to explore without disturbing anything, she gingerly moved deeper under the houses, certain she must be near Miss Scarlet by now.

Goose bumps…

Startled, she crossed her arms and rubbed furiously, but not to be denied, the boulders raged across her shoulders and down her spine.

Someone's here, I feel it—them?

Certain she'd been alone before, she didn't feel alone now. Not—at—all.

Instead, the basement teemed with—what? Energy? Banging? Screams? Whip cracks? Ripped flesh?

Imagination, she chided herself.

As fast as the sounds came, they went. In a blink, the basement once again became quiet as an empty church.

The insulating blanket of snow muted all sounds except wheels spinning down the hill on Central Avenue.

The policemen? That quickly?

Hunched to avoid banging her head or knocking something—or someone—loose, she backtracked towards the stairs. She'd heard the term quiver-in-your-boots before, but this was the first time she remembered doing so.

Remember your Mudras, a familiar voice whispered.

"Andrine? Is that you?"

Andrine lived deep in the swamps of Orange County, Texas. Locals all called her an evil Voodoo woman, but she'd been Sidra's wise counselor on several occasions.

Don't let fear get the best of you. Remember the Ahamkara Mudra—it's the one that counteracts fear and timidity. Don't leave this place without protecting yourself.

Sidra stopped at the bottom of the stairs, breathed in a couple of deep, releasing breaths, then bent her index finger slightly, put the upper part of her thumb to the side of the middle index finger, the other fingers held straight up, and breathed in again, releasing the position of her fingers.

One slow careful step after the other, she felt the stairway rock and creak all the way up. She reached the top and stepped through the doorway, trusting the Mudra to not only renew her confidence, but to counteract any fear that might overtake her sense of reason and security.

"Good lord, where have you been? Did you just walk through a wall or something?" Belle stood at the kitchen sink and had swung around when the floor creaked. All the blood looked drained from her face.

"Is there a door back there?" Sawyer stood in the doorway between the kitchen and the living room. "I didn't see a door or anything that looked vaguely like one?"

"We thought you must have fallen asleep. We didn't check, didn't want to disturb you, but...where have you been?"

"This is crazy," Sidra said, but there is a basement that runs almost the length of these houses, and yes, I found a door down to it."

"What did you find?" They both asked at the same time.

Sidra described what she saw and what she heard, while the other two gaped.

"Really? A skeleton buried under this house?" Belle asked.

"Don't know about a complete skeleton, but fingers to a hand at the very least. No wonder we've seen and felt left behind energies. At least parts of them are buried underneath us. Of course, that still doesn't explain the woman in the house last night, or the other women."

"Women? As in plural?" Sawyer gawked from Sidra to Belle to Sidra. "More than whatever the hell that was sitting on your bed last night crying?"

"We haven't told you what happened before you got here," Belle said.

"You...you haven't? What? What haven't you told me?"

Belle recounted their experiences inside Miss Lilly in the middle of the night.

"I don't believe this...yes, I believe you, but I never believed in ghosts—that is until I saw whatever that was on Sidra's bed."

Curious, Belle went over to the basement door to see for herself, then clicked off the light and closed the door. "What do we do now? Shouldn't we call the police? If someone's been buried under these houses, then—"

"I called the police department while I was downstairs, still looking at the fingers. I wanted to describe what I saw."

"What did they say?" Sawyer asked.

"Better yet, what did you say?" Belle added.

"I told them what I saw, who I was, where we were staying, that sort of thing. Explained I didn't think there was need for a big rush, especially in this weather. Whatever—or whomever it is, they aren't going anywhere. I gave them my cell number and this address. They said they would get here as soon as possible."

Sidra stopped short of sharing any more information on her experience in the basement, at least until she had time to make sense of it all.

An uneasy quiet settled over the room. Cabin fever seemed to be settling in, making all of them restless. Sidra went to the kitchen, poured herself a glass of red wine, and returned to staring out the living room window. Being from southeast Texas, she hadn't experienced snow often. It gave a sense of calm, quiet innocence.

That is until a conversation started up behind her.

"Sawyer," Belle said, "you don't have any idea who the man was that called Maxx? Think back—anyone from your past—anyone at all? Maybe some unanswered questions?

With his elbow propped on the arm of the chair, he leaned forward and said, "I've been wracking my brain going over my life, what I know of it. I know my mother died in prison, murdered by another inmate, they said. My father… What was his name? I read it somewhere in an old photo album or something?" He shrugged, "It's gone."

Sidra moved away from her moment of peace, tossed a throw pillow on the floor, and sat in front of the fireplace, now with a fire blazing—thanks to Sawyer and his Boy Scout skills.

"Okay, let's make notes—I'll jot down what we know. Belle, your mother owned these houses, inherited from her mother, and her mother's mother. This Margaret figures in the whole thing somewhere—especially since Warren said—"

Warren? Damn it, Sidra hadn't intended to tell them about her psychic dead brother—*maybe* dead brother. "Never mind. Some guy—"

"Margaret? Who's Margaret?"

Sidra glanced at Belle, relieved Sawyer hadn't noticed her slip of the tongue, but curious as to how much they should tell him. Evidently Belle felt the same way, because she answered.

"Just a woman we met downtown."

"Oh, okay."

"Let's list all the people we've met since we've been here," Belle said. "Something tells me none of those occurrences have been by accident. I'm even wondering if the finger bones might be a plant."

"A plant? You mean like perhaps they aren't real?"

"Maybe."

"Okay, Belle, how about you starting. I'll write." Sidra scooted closer to the fire.

"First one I think of is this old man I keep seeing walk by, no idea where he lives or where he goes, but I definitely feel a connection with him."

"Yeah, and there's an old woman," Sidra wrote faster. "She spoke to me, called me someone else—what was it? Oh yes, said my name was Miss White, even after I corrected her. That's crazy. Besides, this isn't my story, this is yours, Belle, so why...?"

The list grew longer, while Sidra made notes. Sawyer roamed the floor, commenting from time to time. On one of his trips to the window, he said, "Hey, looks like the storm's passed. The suns coming out and trucks are tossing salt on the streets downtown—one's coming this way—and right behind him is the police."

They stared out the window as the vehicles made their way up the hill towards them.

"Figured they wouldn't make it until tomorrow," Sidra said.

As they watched, the police car spun and skidded, rolled back down, then started up again. They parked on the street below, and two uniformed policemen tromped through the virgin snow, to the steps. The sound of boots knocking off snow reminded Belle to bring an old towel to help keep the frozen mess off the hardwood floor. She tossed it in front of the door and stepped back.

When they knocked, Sidra opened the door to a blast of cold air. Shivering, she invited them in, indicating the rag for their feet.

"Oh, thank you," they both said in unison. "We knocked off as much snow as we could, but we're still a mess."

The shorter of the two stared around the room. He looked like he fulfilled a dream come true. "Never been in these houses before, but heard lots of stories about them."

The taller man reached his hand out to Sidra. "I'm Detective Street, the lead, and this is Detective Taylor. You the one who called and reported the remains of a body in your basement?"

Detective Street, tall, maybe mid-fifties, nice-looking, brown hair, and blue eyes surrounded by *happy* crinkles.

Detective Taylor offered his hand, while Detective Street glanced at a notepad then back up. "You're Ms. Smart, Sidra Smart?"

"Yes, I am." She handed him her business card.

"Oh, so you're a private detective. Intuitive Investigations, it says, and from Texas? What brings you to Hot Springs?"

Instead of answering, Sidra turned and introduced Belle and Sawyer, explaining that Belle owned the property, and Sawyer, was a friend.

"But you're the one that saw the bones? That's what I understand."

"Yes, I accidentally came across the door in the utility room and went exploring—cabin fever, you know." She chuckled.

Did he buy that? He looked like he had, but cops were trained to hide their feelings.

"I see." He made a note on the pad. "Now, can you show me what you saw?"

Chapter Twenty-Three

Sidra turned on the light and led the entourage down the dim, rickety stairs, Detective Street at her heels. His flashlight helped guided them into the abyss, now ever more eerie than it had been before. Unexpected, unidentified bones had a way of doing that.

Flashlight beams bounced off junk piled apparently at random, like the old cane-bottom chair with a big fat hole in the middle, and a rusted-out bucket—castoffs of lost souls.

Yeah, Sis, my bucket's got a hole in it, I can't buy no more beer.

Funny, Warren. Leave it to you to make a joke out of all this.

Across the way, Detective Street perused the basement, but with an occasional look-back. Like he suspected someone else might be there. Someone he didn't see, or didn't want to see.

He motioned to Sidra. "Can you show me what you found down here? Not surprised if there's human bones. These old houses carry lots of history—much of it dark."

Sidra led the way. "It's Belle's property, I'm just here visiting. The two knocked away cobwebs and rounded rotting travel trunks and other piles of trash, to the weather-ravaged wood—no longer a door—and moved it aside. He scanned the mud wall with his flashlight and stopped.

In contrast with the dark mud wall, the bony fingers glowed. Detective Street took a step back, then regrouped and moved to take a closer look.

"Hell, if one looked close enough, one might think they moved—jiggled just a bit." He chuckled and stepped back. "Taylor. Come take a look."

Detective Taylor crossed the dirt floor, looked at the finger bones, whistled, and stepped in for a closer look. "They definitely look human."

Young, maybe late twenties or early thirties, Sidra wondered if he'd ever seen bones like that before. Even in the darkness, his face turned almost as white as the bones sticking out of the hardened dirt. To be honest, hers likely did too when she first saw them. He stepped backward, stumbled, and caught himself on a rusty bicycle frame. "I'll see if I can find anything else."

Detective Street turned to Sid. "I'll have to get an archeological crew in to identify these and see what else might be down here. Would not be surprised, a place as old as this. I need to ask you and your friends to stay out of the area until after we get done. Don't mess with or move anything. You were right to call me right away. Gives us a chance to start clean."

After a cursory look around, the detectives stretched a crime scene tape crisscross the door, admonished them to not cross it, then left, promising they'd hear from them or their boss sometime the next day.

"Hope you two like chili; this kind of weather begs for it." Sidra headed to the fridge and pulled out the makings for a chili supper. Just as she did, the power went off again.

"Good thing there's a gas stove." Sawyer brought a couple of extra candles to the kitchen and lit them. "Anything else I can do to help?"

"See if you can find a few more pieces of wood outside and get a fire going in the fireplace. We can settle around it for a candlelit supper."

While Sidra cooked and Sawyer tended the fire, Belle curled up on the small sofa. By the look on her face, her mind had taken her to another time and place.

Sawyer appeared to notice as well. He kept glancing Belle's way.

"Belle," he finally said, "I want to be your friend—if you'll let me. I know you aren't interested in me physically, romantically, and that's okay. Truth is, I've been forcing interest in you."

Belle's mouth dropped open.

"I know, I've acted otherwise, but truth be known, your father pushed me towards you, despite the objections of your mother. Thought I could get you more interested in church, that sort of thing. I like you, and I've tried to develop romantic feelings, but..." His words trailed off as if deep thought transported him elsewhere. He returned a couple of long minutes later. "But, truth be known, there's nothing there. Well, except I care about you. I didn't mean to imply..."

He looked at his hands, picked at his fingernails. "Might we just be friends? No pressure for anything else—just friends?"

Belle looked stunned, speechless. She stared at him for the longest, her eyes growing clearer, her demeanor softer, lighter.

The forgotten ground meat began to stick to the bottom of the skillet.

Focus, Sidra. Focus.

She pulled her attention back to the task at hand, all while sneaking a frequent look at the other two.

"Yes, let's try that." Belle smiled.

"Excellent," Sawyer said, grinning. "I'd really like to stay and see if I can help you find answers to all these questions, if you and Sidra don't mind. Not that you need me. I get the feeling you two can take care of most anything on your own, but I feel like I've got something invested here, too. Don't ask me what; I haven't the foggiest idea, but…"

"Makes sense—based on what you told me about my father and his watch care, or control, over you. That's him—was him. I wonder how many secrets we'll find."

The evening wore on. Sidra finished the chili and served bowls of it topped with sour cream, and a handful of grated cheese, while they huddled around the fireplace. Still without power, the candles grew shorter and shorter.

No one had spoken for several minutes, until Sawyer broke the silence.

"Well, are the two of you planning to stay up and check on the houses tonight? Going to be mighty cold out there."

"No, not me," Belle pulled a blanket around her. "I don't think so. Let's give it a rest until after the cops come tomorrow. No telling what all that's going to entail. Or what they might find. I'm curious as to who is buried down there, or if they are—could just be finger bones."

"Maybe Miss Lilly, the woman in the yellow dress." The words popped out of Sidra's mouth without foreknowledge.

"Maybe—could be." Belle spooned more sour cream on top of the grated cheese then took another bite of chili, "Good stuff," she said as she blew on the steaming bowl.

"Meanwhile, I'm trying to guess who that man was that was hit by the hit-and-run driver in Houston, and why he was looking for me." Sawyer finished his first bowl and headed back for more.

They sat in silence again, each lost in their own thoughts. Until the stairs leading to the bedrooms creaked a couple of times. Like someone had been upstairs and now came down to join them.

Chapter Twenty-Four
Miss Fancy

Will nothing work? Will nothing make them leave us alone? We grow more desperate, my sisters and I. Tricks we used before were always successful in driving folks away so we might rest in peace. What is it about these that now make them immune to our best efforts? Must we grow bolder? Must we pull out a different bag of tricks?

Scarlet, brazen Scarlet, thought her tricks might work. Lilly thought if she paid the older one a visit, that might work.

All to no avail.

Now they find bones, not the last bones they will find should they dig.

My sisters say we must take more drastic measures to rid ourselves of them.

However, I stand in opposition to that. My thoughts now turn to revealing ourselves to them, soliciting their help in freeing us from this hell. A hell we innocents continue to pay the price for, yet were, and are victims in our own rights. Some *thing*…or some *one* yells at me, words I cannot understand, yet ring true. Smells overtake me. Horrid smells, putrid, decaying, hideous, stomach churning.

Something about this young man—Sawyer, they call him—informs me he holds the key. The lines of his chin, his high cheekbones appear familiar—like they belong here—or did—eons ago. The darkness that hovers just outside his aura hints at secrets yet to be revealed.

Lilly fears the identity of the bones—fingers from our past—might well bring retribution on us—not due to guilt, but due to kept secrets.

Secrets, yes, but secrets to save our souls.

Or so we thought. Yet our souls cry out for salvation even now.

We must be brave, braver than ever. Denying them admittance has not helped. Perhaps the truth—the whole truth—shall set us free, and in the doing, perhaps that freedom might be shared.

Perhaps our presence, not as figments illuminated in the middle of the night, but as fellow travelers. It is obvious they care. They are not here to *ghost hunt*. They come for answers, especially the younger woman. Belle, they call her. She holds the key—the connection.

The Sawyer man, we sense a different connection. His pain is much deeper. In another lifetime, he suffered greatly, and when he came back, at least in this lifetime, those pains came with him. As a result, he is yet unfinished, the marvel of his creation torn asunder, broken into pieces, leaving great holes in his past, yet no one sees them—not even him.

This woman they call Belle is unfinished as well, and caught in the sins of past lifetimes, and those inflicted on her in this one. She has seen much pain. Experienced even more. Hers came much after—yet when broken bits of pain are left to float in the ethers, it lands on those most vulnerable, bounces around unstoppable, until the wounds of past are made clear. Until then, she will struggle to be herself and feel no one wants her for such. Until she accepts herself, she will find trouble wherever she goes.

Now the older woman—*Miss White*—her connection intertwines theirs, yet goes much deeper—so much deeper. She is like a rag doll—not real, yet not unreal. A prior lifetime wounded her core, not because of what she did, but because of what she could not do.

We alone know the truth, not out of wisdom, but of experience. I see it now, clearer than ever before. Our wounds infiltrate theirs. Their wounds infiltrate ours. We cannot escape the pains of the other.

Wounded healers: Our escape. Our task. Our honor.

Only that saves us.

I must hurry now to find my sisters.

Chapter Twenty-Five

The cold front moved out overnight, and by the next morning, the temperature resumed a more seasonal level. The sun came out and the ice and snow soon turned to slush. Belle and Sawyer complained that they hadn't slept any better than Sidra. They too experienced mysterious images, noises, odd feelings, voices, and chill bumps all night. Even Slider hadn't settled down until just before sunrise.

With all the noises in Sidra's head, or dreams, when she did sleep, she felt unsure where reality started and where it stopped.

Or if it did.

Belle made the first pot of coffee extra strong, evident her feelings and nighttime experiences had taken a toll. All three of them seemed reluctant to discuss anything other than—*more coffee, please*—until midmorning when the sound of car tires fighting their way up the hill caused a rush to the windows.

"Police, again." Sidra gulped the last of her coffee and rinsed her cup.

Belle left hers on the coffee table. "Yep," she said. "One marked and one unmarked. Looks like Detective Street's driving one of them."

She opened the door before the first knock. "Come in. We figured you might show up this morning." She motioned them inside.

"Good morning, again." Detective Street indicated the others. "This is Detective Carroll; she usually heads up these kinds of investigations, and Palmer, here."

Palmer, a small, dark, intense-looking man, carried a small leather bag, zipped tight. He stepped inside and rested it near the door. Something inside the bag clanged.

Detective Street spoke to Sidra, but his eyes focused over her head, in the direction of the yellow crime scene tape across the basement door. "You all doing okay?"

"Yes, and the tape has not been touched." Sidra hoped he heard the smile in her voice. One thing she didn't want was to piss off the police. "We followed your orders. No one has been down since you left." A laugh slipped out with her words. "Actually, no one *wanted* to go down."

"Good morning." Sawyer shook hands with the officers.

"I've filled Detective Carroll in, she's—" Static, then a voice on Detective Street's shoulder mic interrupted him. "Excuse me, let me get this." He stepped back out to the front porch.

Detective Carroll stepped forward. Short and solid, she sported a mass of long, thick black curls bound at the nape. She wore solid black pants and a jacket. Although she looked all business, something about her spoke to Sidra. Her aura looked pure. Clean.

"I'm Belle Anderson. We figured you'd be here this morning soon as the roads cleared. As I explained to Detective Street, I recently inherited this property from my mother, who…passed recently, she and my father. I had no idea she owned them. That's why we're here. I asked Sidra to come with me. I'd like to fix up the property and sell it—maybe."

"Nice to meet all of you." Detective Carroll shook hands with each. Her voice, deep and resonate hinted of authenticity and stability. "Which one is the private eye?" She looked from Sidra to Sawyer.

"Not me," Sawyer said, chuckling.

"Then that leaves you, Ms. Smart." She turned to Belle. "So let me understand, Miss Anderson, why a private detective?" She pulled out a paper and pen and started making notes. "Did you suspect something might be out of order?"

Sidra half expected Belle to say something about a life out of order, but she didn't.

"I've known Ms. Smart for years. Her husband—ex-husband—was a peer of my father's. Since I had no clue about this property, and the whole thing was handled so… so…"

"So what?"

"Mysteriously, I guess, is the word. Seems my parents kept all this secret for years—my mother inherited it from her family, but my father, he…"

Belle's eyes glistened with moisture. Her voice cracked.

"Okay, I get the picture. You wanted Ms. Smart to accompany you, more as a friend than a PI. Right?"

Belle nodded. "Yes, that's about it."

"How about you, Mr. Sawyer? Did you come with them?"

Sawyer ducked his head. "I… I got worried about Belle when she didn't answer my calls, so I drove over."

Carroll glanced at Belle. "His calls didn't come

through?"

"I didn't answer them."

"I see." The officer scribbled notes on her pad. "Okay, enough about that."

Carroll glanced up when Detective Street came back inside then looked over at Sidra. "Detective Street says you're the one who first found the bones, Ms. Smart. Were you suspicious of anything? What made you go exploring a dark basement in the midst of a November snowstorm?"

"Antsy, I guess," Sidra said, snorting.

"Antsy? Over what?

"Weird dreams and odd occurrences left me feeling—"

"Odd occurrences?"

Sidra cut a quick look at Belle then cursed her own lack of control. She'd lay odds Carroll hadn't missed it, and Sidra wasn't sure she wanted to talk about what she'd seen and heard—not yet, at least. "I don't really know how to explain it, but…"

Detective Carroll cleared her throat. "Err, well, you may not know it, but these houses have a reputation for *odd occurrences*, as you call it. People say they're haunted. Whether that's true or not, I can't say—but they *are* on the *Haunted Hot Springs Tour*. Likely the reason why the property can't keep tenants for long." She turned to Belle. "You say your mother and her family owned these houses? For how long?"

"Generations."

"Really? Then that would mean—"

Street put his hand up to Carroll. "Let's not get into all of that right now," he said. "It doesn't concern the investigation. We need to stay focused on—"

"Oh, of course." She laughed. You'll have to excuse me, seems I was born a story catcher. I can get carried away by tales from the past."

"That's okay. At least we know we're not crazy."

Sidra glanced from Belle to Sawyer.

"Detective Street is right, however. Our concerns are the bones you found in the basement. If you would pardon us for a few minutes, he will show me where they are, and we will likely do a little excavating, dig around a bit."

"Sure," Belle said. "Are we to wait up here?"

"Yes, please. We don't want anything disturbed."

The third person, Palmer, picked up the small bag he'd rested on the floor. Again, the bag clanged.

Detective Street pointed Carroll to the small laundry room door and removed the crime scene tape. One of them pulled the light cord, and they headed down the rickety stairs.

Meanwhile, Belle, Sawyer, and Sidra stared at each other.

That is until Dr. Carroll eased back up the stairs, bustling into the kitchen, looking behind her as if she didn't want the others to know she'd come back upstairs.

"Ms. Smart," she whispered, "this isn't police business, but it sure might fit in with what you're trying to accomplish with these houses."

"What is it? I'm open to any ideas."

"There's this woman who lives out from town a little ways." Carroll looked over her shoulder again, lowered her voice. "She *knows things* other people don't—if you get my meaning. Calls herself a witch, only in jest, you understand, but she's different, that's for sure. Honest as the day is long. If it were me, I'd call and see if she might set up a time to talk."

"What's her name? How do we find her?" Carroll's suggestion had definitely engaged Sidra's curiosity.

"Here," she pulled a white card out of her wallet, handed it to Sidra, and headed back down the basement steps, calling out, "Tell I sent you."

"What's that all about," Belle asked.

Sidra felt all the blood drain from her face when she read the name given her.

"Ravina Nation, isn't…isn't she the one we met at—"

"At the pancake shop, yes, it is. The same one who acted so weird when she heard about the sister houses."

After what seemed an eternity, but in reality maybe a couple of minutes, they heard a sound from the front and peered out the window. Palmer opened the hatch of the SUV parked behind the other cars, retrieved a couple of shovels, and returned to the rear of the house.

Minutes later, Street came upstairs, headed to the unmarked car, and retrieved what looked to be a camera bag.

Tension inside the house built with each tick of the clock.

Close to noon, they heard the officers coming up the stairs, chatting among themselves but nothing distinguishable. By the time they reached the top, Sidra, Belle, and Sawyer stood waiting.

Detective Carroll stepped forward. "Ms. Smart, our forensic archeologist here," pointing to Palmer," has identified the bones you found as human—likely female."

No one spoke for a couple of seconds.

"What's next?" Sidra asked.

"Well, it seems there is more going on than a couple of finger bones. We excavated a little deeper and discovered those finger bones were actually connected to what looks like a skeleton—we haven't gotten that far in yet, so not sure, but… They did a little more excavating, and at first glance, it seems those are not the only bones buried in the basement.

"Until we can do further exploration, we have no idea what might be buried there. Palmer here uncovered several more, and my fear is that we only scratched the surface. Some of the bones—well—they look human, but small—almost as if…well, let's wait until we know more."

"I see. I had a feeling… I…there's no telling what…" Belle's voice quivered and stopped.

"Where does that put us?" Sidra picked up the

conversation. "Must we leave the premises?"

"Oh no, at least not at this point. But the basement is off-limits for everyone but our officers and crew."

The team moved towards the front door, and then Jeffries stopped and turned. "Oh, by the way, we did find another entry."

"Where?" Sidra felt sure she'd done a thorough checking of the area.

Some private detective you turned out to be.

Shut up, Warren.

"Don't feel bad if you didn't see it. Our officers almost missed it, too. It's blocked by a strategic placement of bushes planted close to the house. Over the years, they've grown so big it blocks all view. We've taped it off. We're also going to check for tunnels. Palmer knows a lot about all the tunnels underneath this town, and he—well, we'll see. You can walk back there and check it out, just make sure you don't disturb anything."

"We won't," Sawyer said.

"Tomorrow, Palmer will have a crew here, and they'll start excavating. We hope to keep this out of the news as best we can, but in case anyone asks you what's going on, refer them to our Public Relations department."

After the officers left, Slider and Jenkins were allowed outside to plunder the neighborhood while the dazed trio went out for lunch. They picked a local pizza place alongside the lake and sat near a window overlooking the water.

Their orders placed, they each stared at the other as though afraid to speak, or had no words to say.

Sidra broke the silence. "Okay, folks. We have got to get ourselves together or this is going to keep us all awake. We have no idea what happened here in the past, and I've never believed spirits walk this earth—or used to believe such, but right now, events lead me to doubt that belief. It also leads me to believe anything is possible. Maybe these *things* we see are beginning to add up."

"But why? How? And what does this have to do with my mother and her ancestors?"

"That's the big question."

Sawyer stared out at the lake. He looked like his thoughts were a million miles away.

"Where did you go, Sawyer?" Belle asked.

"Sorry," he said, laughing.

"That's okay," Belle put her hand on his shoulder. "Just take us with you."

"I just had this flashback. When I was a kid, I'd sit around and listen to people talk about the mafia and how Hot Springs became a vacation spot for them. I'd forgotten all about that till just now. New York, Chicago, the whole bit."

"I can tell you how to learn more about it. The first morning Sidra and I were here, I noticed a Gangster Museum downtown on Central Avenue."

Sawyer's mouth dropped.

The next morning Sawyer and Belle took his car and headed downtown to the Gangster Museum while Sidra found the address of the Garland County Library and plugged it into her phone GPS.

It took a few minutes to find a parking place. An active public library always spoke well of any town—in her opinion. Local art of various types and styles impressed her. On the right, a colorful, fun-looking children's library was full to overflowing with preschoolers and their parents.

She located the area dedicated to books of local interest and browsed. The Historical Society members had been active and prolific.

A cursory glance of books revealed Hot Springs had a colorful and sometimes dangerous past. From being the home of the first all-black baseball team, the first home of

Spring Training for various baseball teams, and not to mention the spas. One book, *Bathhouse Row: We Bathe The World*, intrigued her. She laid it aside for further study. Top of her to-do list would be one of those spas on Bathhouse Row. After, she reminded herself, they got to the bottom of the mysteries of the three houses. Their history, what, when, how?

She moved down the row of books. *Arkansas Godfather: The Story of Owney Madden and How He Hijacked Middle America.*

Another, *Dangerous Visitors: The Lawless Era.* Now that one might offer an event that connected to the houses.

The Mob at the Spa: Organized Crime and Its Fascination with Hot Springs—getting closer. The cover of the book pictured Al Capone's bulletproof 1928 Cadillac.

She'd always thought of Hot Springs as a tourist area due to the lakes and hot mineral springs but had not realized its reputation as the vacation spot for gangsters.

Her mind wandered to what gangsters brought to a town. Definitely lawlessness. Seems the town had its share of such. One book looked to be authored by the Madame who owned and ran several *houses* in the early 1900s.

She flipped to the first page of *The Mob at the Spa.*

Soon she found herself flipping through the pages to discover a long list of gangsters who were frequented the area. Not only the well-known Al Capone but also Owney Madden, called the Arkansas Godfather, Charles Dion O'Bannion, Albert Anastasia, called The Lord High Executioner, Frank Costello, Arnold Rothstein…on and on the list grew.

Thumbing through the pages, it was evident Hot Springs was the vacation spot for the mafia. The authorities took payoffs and looked the other way while the gangsters walked the streets of the town in total safety.

One writer described how Al Capone laid claim to the whole fourth floor of the large Arlington Hotel when he came to town. They treated him like royalty. Underground tunnels provided him easy access to brothels, bars, and other hangouts.

Good lord. Lawlessness approved by local law enforcement officers. Payoffs resulted in little to no enforcement of prostitution laws.

Is that what led to wandering spirits in Belle's houses? Were they indeed brothels? Is that why her father refused to talk about the property? Now that the houses were listed in the historical registry, Lillian Anderson could not have torn them down, but she could have sold them.

Or were there other reasons her mom kept them, passed down from generation to generation? Yes, Sid could understand the generational ties—but what else might connect them? Why had so many moved in over the years only to shortly move out? Could it be the spirits walking the halls? Or had something else happened?

Enough to keep her busy for days, she thought. Too bad she couldn't check them out—or could she?

"Might I see the library director?" Sidra asked at the large round bar that sat in the middle of the main lobby.

"Sure, let me see if I can find him."

Soon, a tall attractive white-haired man with a friendly smile approached. After introducing himself, he asked how he could help.

Sidra handed him her *Third Eye, Intuitive Investigations* business card. "I'm here in town with a client who recently inherited the three houses up on Court Street. Unknown to her, it seems they've been in her mother's family for several generations. She'd like to get a little more history, not only on them but also on the town. Is there any way I might borrow these books," she indicated the ones in her hands. "I can leave a deposit or whatever you require. I promise I won't leave town without returning them."

His dark blue eyes peered into hers for the longest,

looking through to not only her character but also her soul. At least it felt that way.

"I'll tell you what. I don't usually do this—fact is I'm not sure I ever have, but I'm going to check them out on my card, and let you have them—for how long? Maybe a couple of weeks?"

"Oh, less than that. I'll get right on them. With this weather, I'm not likely to do much else."

He grabbed a pen from his shirt pocket, made note of the titles, stapled her business card to the note, and put it in his pocket. "I know where you live—here and in Texas—so let's do this."

"Thank you. I'll get them back to you in a couple of days."

See, Sis, sometimes you have not because you ask not. Good girl.

"Shut up, Warren," she whispered as she climbed in the car. "What is it about big brothers who always try to convince their baby sisters they know so much more?"

Because we do.

By the time she pulled into the driveway, a host of cars, some marked, others unmarked, but official nonetheless, lined the street. She exited and noticed a path already worn through the melting snow around to the rear of the house. After depositing the books inside, she left by the front door and followed the path around the house.

Hard-packed dirt lay in piles atop black plastic bags. Several people she hadn't seen before came and went, ignoring her. Yellow crime tape roped off most of the back yard. Shrubs that had surrounded the outside entry now sat in large black containers, protected, she assumed, for replacement.

As she turned to retrace her steps, Forensic Archeologist Carroll walked up behind her. "Hello, Ms.

Smart," she indicated the back yard. "Kind of a mess right now, but we'll fix it when we're done."

Sidra smiled. "A big job, it looks like. Why the piles of dirt?"

"One of the most important aspects of my job is for my team to perform controlled recovery of any human remains we find, plus, any other evidence that a forensic anthropologist might need to make an accurate conclusion of the remains. Who, what, when, and where kind of thing—to put it in lay terms."

"Fascinating. I think I might have missed my calling." Sidra smiled.

"Actually, I'm not sure that's accurate. If it were not for you, we would not be here. These houses are over a hundred years old. Many residents have come and gone, but no one ever reported bony fingers." She paused and then said, "As a matter of fact, I don't recall the ownership ever-changing, and you know how renters come and go."

"What are you finding?"

"Let me put it this way. Enough human remains to fill a small graveyard."

"What?"

Carroll nodded. "And if I know my job like I think I do, they were not all buried at the same time—maybe not even in the same generation…"

Sidra's mouth dropped open.

Chapter Twenty-Six
Miss Fancy

"I *understand* your desire, Lilly," I say, "and your intent is honorable, I suppose. Yet we alone are left as witnesses to events on this once sacred land—this *place of peace.*"

The derision in my voice strikes its intended mark. Many times Lilly has heard me speak of the original inhabitants of this land and of how all the hostile tribes agreed this sacred land—this *Valley of Vapors*—remain a place of peace. Warring might occur outside the sacred valley, but not within, where generous springs offered its hot mineral waters for healing to all who came.

"Our very presence amidst the destruction of that peace you often speak about binds us here as surely as if we were co-conspirators." I continue my argument against aiding the most recent residents. "Yet we turned not our hand to commit such evil perpetrated behind these walls, only served as mere witnesses."

My turquoise skirt and billowing petticoats swoosh, as I pace from room to room, walls no barrier to my path. "Father was not alone in his wickedness. Many came after, yet we are the ones bound here for eternity."

Lilly looks in deep thought. I allow her the time to defend her unwillingness to help the boarders before I speak further.

"You also speak truth when you say, should they stay, their wounds shall infiltrate ours, and our wounds, theirs. That is most precisely why we cannot let them stay."

Lilly swishes to the sofa and sits beside Scarlet, the baby of the family, and the most rebellious. Scarlet reclines on the sofa, dressed in what father always called *full-whore-regalia*, looking bored with it all.

"What do you think, Scarlet?" Lilly asks. "Might you, for once in your life, pay attention to something other than yourself? Stop fiddling with that hair and tell Fancy and me what you think we should do? Our usual tricks, or…?"

"Evil still permeates our walls," Scarlet says. "You know that, but have we not found ways to protect ourselves? Is life here so bad that we must—"

"Yes, my dear sister, but when is enough, enough?" I mount my case against the opposition. "Haven't we earned our rest? Might we move on in the afterlife? I do not know about you, but a century or more trapped in this place feels long enough. I have a feeling if we fail to help these folks, we may never get out. The houses will one day fall down, but that doesn't mean the wicked spirits will abandon their entrenchment."

Scarlet ignores Lilly and I. Instead, she snatches a nearby hand mirror, peers in, and pouts. "I've been checking for my reflection in this thing for close to a hundred years. You'd think I'd learn mirrors don't work for me anymore. I miss seeing my pretty face and my scarlet hair. Sure glad Mama insisted on naming me that.

It fits, don't you think? I always liked the boys begging to touch it." She frowns and tosses the mirror on the sofa. "Now, they run away screaming."

I ignore the whining. One grows callous of such vain self-commentary.

As is her habit in most anything that doesn't fit her opinion, Lilly lifts her chin, and, haughty, turns her back, and stomps off in defense of her position. "I see no reason to alter our ways—no reason whatso—"

"Whatsoever, what?" I ask, exasperated with the two of them.

"Well, I so happen to agree with Lilly," Scarlet blasts, adding a trail of curse words.

I cringe, wondering once again, if not for Scarlet's rebellious nature, perhaps Father would not have gone on such a rampage that day. Not that he had any right to judge his youngest daughter. His crimes were far more severe than her snuggling up to every boy needing a poke.

"We've got new problems," I say, peering out the window. "Why are strange men coming out of our basement carrying heavy-looking black bags?"

Chapter Twenty-Seven

Police excavations completed and crime scene tape removed, Sawyer took advantage of a warmer day and went outside to tend his neglected automobile. He pulled out a water hose, cleaned off mud and leftover chunks of snow and ice under the fenders, and checked the oil and antifreeze, all while recent events puddled in his mind. He'd never expected to be involved in such a mess when he'd left Texas. As far as he knew, authorities hadn't identified any of the bones.

As he slammed the hood, his cell phone vibrated. He wiped his hands on a greasy red rag and pulled out the phone.

"Sawyer, here. Yes, but who did you say this is? Oh, Maxx! Didn't recognize your voice. What's up?"

By the time he rang off, he felt like he'd been hit in

the gut by a prizefighter. He half stumbled up the steps and flopped onto the front steps.

Seems Houston PD identified the man looking for him, the same man struck and killed by a hit and run driver later that same day. Seems the person was a lawyer from another state—Arkansas, actually. Seems they found the driver and the man confessed. Seems the drunk driver was already on probation for more than one DWI, but the police investigation revealed information the lawyer had on his body at the time of the accident. Information for Sawyer, and it had something to do with an inheritance of property in, of all places, Hot Springs, Arkansas. Maxx said he'd thought it all an odd coincidence, given Belle's current situation.

How in the world could Sawyer explain this to Belle? Sidra was a private eye. Perhaps she could put the pieces together.

Sidra walked outside, Slider at her heels. Agitation had ridden high on the shoulders of both dogs over the last few days. What with all the night visitors, day visitors, and cops, both Slider and Jenkins seemed on edge. They skulked around with their hackles raised. Sawyer understood the feeling. Hairs on his neck and arms too stood at alert.

"The car looks nice." Sidra walked over and sat next to him. "I need to get out here and work on Belle's."

"Never mind that, I'll get it cleaned up and checked out."

"Oh, thanks, that's nice of you."

"I had a call from Maxx right before you came out. A puzzling call."

"Oh? What now?" Sidra pulled her sweater tighter.

"Seems the police did some follow-up on the hit-and-run accident that killed the guy looking for me."

"Intentional?"

"Doesn't seem so—not that they can tell—however, what did boggle my mind is they learned why the victim was looking for me."

Sidra turned to face Sawyer. "Really?"

"It sounds so…"

"Trite?"

"Unbelievable, is more like it. Way too coincidental."

"What? Why?"

"Seems the guy had information on property he thought I might be an heir to."

"Oh good lord," Sidra said, laughing. "Don't tell me you need to go check on that, now? Where is it—no doesn't matter. Belle and I can hold the fort here. You go do what you need to do."

Sawyer kicked a clod of icy mud. "That's just it. I don't need to go elsewhere. I'm already there."

"I don't understand."

"The property is right here, in Hot Springs."

"That's convenient. We can check it out. Guess you have the details or the contact person…?"

"Yep." He tried to squash a grin because it wasn't funny—more ironic. "Seems there's a vacant lot next door to these three houses in a row—on Court Street."

Sidra stared at him—unblinking. He wasn't even sure she breathed.

"You're kidding me!"

Sawyer laughed, "Not on your life."

"I don't understand. You mean to tell me you—you—are part owner of this property?" She waved her arm to include all three houses. Slider yapped and ran around in circles until Sidra grabbed his collar and rubbed him soothingly. "It's okay, babe. We're okay," she said, lowering her voice, to what she hoped sounded reassuring. She doubted her success.

"I don't know about the part, more like adjacent to them."

"Oh, good lord…"

"You two got your heads together about something." Belle called from the doorway. "What's going on?"

Sawyer looked at Sidra. "What do we do now?"

"We tell Belle."

"Detective Carroll called while you two were outside," Belle said as soon as they stepped in the house. "They have no idea the identity of the bones but did say they are all very old—like a hundred years or so, some even older than that. They will be checking old files, but have little to go on and are not optimistic at this point. Said they were turning the specimens over to the state crime lab."

Sawyer knelt beside Belle and took her hands in his. "Maxx called."

He repeated the same story to Belle as he'd told Sidra.

After sitting speechless for several minutes, Belle looked from Sidra to Sawyer. "I don't understand."

"We don't either," Sidra pulled her chair closer to Belle. "The plot—well, it thickens, for sure. I can't help but think these—these—women we see in the middle of the night might be the only way we are ever going to find out anything. Either that, or you can just sell the homes, and Sawyer can sell the lot next door and be done with it—get on with your lives."

"But Sawyer can't have inherited this property—we aren't kin, and Maxx said these have been handed down from generation to… Did he explain that to you, Sawyer?"

Sawyer shook his head. "I'm as confused as you."

Belle continued. "They can't be worth very much, especially since it seems the whole town is scared of them—or of what walks the halls at night, but…"

Sidra, you know what you must do.

"What?" Sidra demanded, exasperated at her nagging brother.

"What, what?" Belle and Sawyer both looked at her, wide-eyed.

"Sorry. Just…just…trying to…"

Trying to get out of it, I know.

Trying to get out of it my eye, Sidra said, but this time, only to herself. No reason to upset the other two by admitting her meddlesome dead brother sometimes got on her last nerve.

You must meet with the sisters. They have all the answers—and thanks to my—what you call interference—I think they are ready to work together to get this situation brought to a conclusion.

Oh good lord, how did she do that—how did she *dare* do that?

Warren, if you're telling me to have séance, you're crazy. I'm not calling people from the dead. That stuff is hogwash. I'm not a medium.

You don't have to call them, baby sister. They are already here. They have been, for decades. Waiting.

For what? Me?

For you, for somebody—anybody.

What do I do, light candles or something?

From the other side, she heard Warren suck through his teeth.

"Sidra? Sidra? Are you okay?" Belle placed her hand on Sidra's, while Sawyer pushed a glass of water her way.

"What? No, yes, no…I'm fine, it's that—my mind, my mind got to wandering…or something."

"It sure did. You looked far away." Belle rubbed Sidra's shoulder. "You were mumbling something, but I didn't understand what you said."

Gotta be more careful, baby sister. They'll think you're crazy. A chuckle sounded off in the distance then slowly faded away.

"Okay. Here's the deal." She sucked in a deep breath then exploded her next words. "We are going to have a séance."

"A what?" Sawyer and Belle spoke in unison.

"Hey, it took all the courage I had to say it the first time. Don't make me say it again."

"How many of these have you done?" Belle asked.

"Hmmm, let me see, tonight, and one more will make two for me."

Belle and Sawyer stared from her to each other and then back again.

"Do you know how?"

"No idea."

"How do you prepare—before tonight that is? Don't you think you might—"

"What? Study up on it?"

Belle laughed. "Yeah, that's what I was about to suggest."

"I plan to."

"How?"

"I'm going inside right now to Google it." She turned and marched inside, fearful they would follow and notice her hands shake as she booted up the computer and typed in her search question. Within 49 seconds up came 198,000 links. She clicked on the top link and printed out the steps—all eleven of them.

Don't worry, little sister. You have lots of time to prepare. Follow the steps—oh, and by the way, if you notice the first one—must have at least three people present—that's perfect. Three is a trio and four is a crowd—so don't expect to see me tonight.

Yeah, right, that fits. Abandon me right when I need you. I don't have a clue what I'm doing.

Won't be able to say that after tonight. I'll check with you later and see how it went. Oh, and by the way, have the séance in Miss Scarlet. I'll make sure the door is unlocked.

Damn it, Warren. You do this to me every time!

She collected the pages and began to read.

Chapter Twenty-Eight

Nightfall came earlier than Sidra hoped—she guessed séances could be conducted during the day, but the spirits roaming these houses seemed to prefer wee hours of the morning. She felt relief Warren had not instructed her to hold the session in the basement—where any number of spirits hung extra heavy already, and likely waiting for just such an event.

You got it, baby sister. These folks have been waiting a long time to tell their story. Just be careful who you let in.

Meaning?

Meaning sometimes beings seem to come through in sequence, and they all affect the environment a little differently. Usually, the procession calms down depending on the leader and a predominant spirit. Some come through softly, some not so much. It's important that you and Belle maintain control over who comes in and who doesn't.

Okay, you're scaring me.

Don't mean to, but sometimes rogue, chaotic spirits come in expressing anger, hatred. Sometimes these can be demons knocking on the barrier between worlds that hold them away from us.

Thanks a lot.

I'm just saying...

With Sawyer, they met the minimum of three. If she counted Slider and Jenkins, that made five. The article she'd read online said that the leader must be intuitive. Warren insisted she was, and in time, she'd begun to think perhaps he'd been at least half-right. But a séance—where those who had passed over showed up and spoke to the group or the leader, who then shared the information or messages to the others?

The whole idea scared the hell out of her. What if she opened a portal, if indeed such a thing existed, then couldn't get it closed?

Yep, you're on track, baby sister, you're the medium they come through, but Belle, as leader must protect who comes in and who doesn't. The medium is the actual receiver and conduit. The leader supports and protects the medium while in trance, and is there to calm and stabilize the physical experience of the participants.

At least Warren confirmed she was on the right track. She breathed a little easier.

Which didn't last long.

Watch out for chaotic rogue spirits. They're hard to control. Depends on their strength and how bad they want what they want. It can be a real battle, the leader on the outside, and the medium who is essentially under attack from the inside. Rogues are what make séance dangerous.

A raging fireball swelled in her gut. Yes, Belle was a good choice for leader. She would display strength and ability to bolster Sidra's. She stuck her head out the door and called Belle and Sawyer inside.

"Okay, I think this is how we are going to work it. I will serve as the medium, and Belle, I need you to serve as the leader."

"You mean oversee who comes in and who doesn't?"

"Exactly. If we are successful at this, we need to be prepared to protect ourselves."

Sidra focused on Belle. "Seems like you know more about séances than you've said."

"Sat in on one or two, but nothing really happened. No one came through. From what I've heard, that happens a lot of the time. Plus," she added, laughing, "PKs don't often talk about things like that."

"We're going to have the séance inside Miss Scarlet," Sidra said.

"Really? Well, I'm up for it," Sawyer said. "I don't know about you two, but I've about had enough basement."

Belle, who had been looking at Sawyer, spun around to face Sidra. "Really? How? We've never gotten those doors unlocked."

"You'll just have to trust me, for now. The doors will be… Trust me."

Nausea raged in Sidra's gut the remainder of the day. She'd never felt such fear. The living? Yeah, she'd take her chances with most anyone, but the dead come to haunt? Her imagination ran wild when she thought about rogue spirits. She'd never heard of such, but the thought scared her as surely as some of Sam's old sermons when he attempted to bring down the wrath of an angry God. She shuddered from the memory, thankful to be out of that marriage.

It felt like hives rampaged beneath her skin—or was it spiders? The way her chest felt, they must be there too.

By nightfall, all three of them were jittery. Since sleep didn't appear to be an option for any of them, they kept returning to the living room and sitting quietly, no one saying much.

Slider and Jenkins apparently sensed something was up. They both lay on the floor in the middle of the small living room, averting their eyes to follow whoever moved, and then followed their return. Jenkins, on occasion, shot a consulting look at Slider, who snorted, nose flaring.

In time, Sidra noticed her breathing synchronized with Belle and Sawyer's. It grew slower, soft, barely audible. The sound of the clock's ticks and tocks gave a menacing reminder that the hour of reckoning approached.

Warren, where are you? Sidra begged in silence. *You got us into this, and now you are a no-show.*

They sat in Miss Fancy and awaited three a.m.

Warren told Sidra the portals were likely wider open for spirits from the other side around that time. She had difficulty buying any of that nonsense, but this didn't seem to be the time to debate that topic.

Meanwhile, Belle and Sawyer attempted small talk about how in the world they might be connected.

Sidra wondered what the evening could potentially reveal, and if anything related to Sawyer's recent discovery might be uncovered? The timing and the overlap of it all blew her mind.

Might those rogue spirits Warren talked about blunder their way into the séance with mischievous intent, and if so, how would they identify those entities and those that were not?

"I can't believe I'm doing this," Sidra whispered ever so softly, just in case ears she couldn't see listened.

The clock struck two-thirty. Sidra stood, straightened her sweater, and nudged her jeans in place. "Okay, let's go get things set up."

"That is if we can get inside." Belle sounded unconvinced.

"If we can get in, yes. If we can't, well…"

Like actors in a silent movie, they moved through the room donning jackets, collecting their assigned articles, and then filed out the door—slow-motion toy soldiers.

Down the steps, circling the porch to the front yard, past Miss Lilly, and on to Miss Scarlet. The selfish new moon offered not a hint of light. A blast of unseasonably hot air gave warning that they controlled nothing. Sidra carried a huge flashlight, Belle, a bowl of rice as an offering to what spirits may come, and Sawyer, the bag of candles, matches, lighters, essential oils, a few herbs tossed in at the last minute, and anything else they thought they might need—and hoped they didn't.

Jenkins and Slider walked alongside them, but on occasion, each stopped and looked around checking for shadows, she figured, then tucked their ears, ducked their heads, and continued.

Sidra led the way up the steps and stopped at the door. Could she open it? If not, could Belle? She stared at the round black knob, feeling the eyes of the other two who stood behind her staring as well.

Sidra reached for the doorknob and turned.

Nothing.

She increased her grip and twisted. An electric charge radiated up her fingers, to her wrists, passed her elbow, and all the way up her shoulder, where it seemed to stop and reverse to her fingers. It all happened so fast she wondered if she hadn't imagined it. "It looks—and feels like—it doesn't want me to go first. You try, Belle."

She moved over for Belle, who turned the knob without issue, swung the door open, and motioned Sidra to lead the way.

Sidra approached the doorway with more confidence than she felt.

At least they let Belle in—and Sidra hit a brick wall. "Damn!"

"What is it, Sid?" Belle grabbed Sidra's shoulders to

steady her.

"I must be going crazy. I don't see a thing, but something is certainly blocking my way. You try."

Belle slipped across Miss Scarlet's threshold while holding Sidra's hand, and neither had any problem getting inside. Meanwhile, Sawyer waited on the porch.

"What about me?" he called out.

"See if you can come in," Sid said and yanked on a string connected to a dangling light bulb.

"Not a chance. I'll wait out here until you get things under control."

The women laughed. "Wuss!"

"Damn right, I am." Incredulity colored his voice.

"Okay, let's see what we've got." Sidra and Belle perused the room. "It looks different than when we looked inside the other night. Look at all this stuff."

Over to the side, a round wooden table supported four chairs stacked on top. Yellowed newspapers lay in large, dusty piles. A rough-hewn bookshelf leaned towards the dangling light bulb. A bulb chose that moment to go out, then on again, and then grew brighter. The effect left the environment shadowed—confined, claustrophobic.

Some unseen—or unheard—signal sounded an alarm, and they each stopped at the exact same moment. Sidra looked questioningly at Belle, but said not a word, for no word came close to explaining the creepiness sliding down her spine and dripping onto the faded red-flowered carpet. Motionless, she stared at the carpet until the feeling passed, but as it did, odors replaced it. Faint at first, the odors grew stronger the longer she stood there. A whiff of baby powder overpowered her and then coalesced into cigarette smoke, then Evening in Paris perfume, then sweating bodies, shit and rotting flesh-all rolled into one nasty stink bomb. She grabbed her nose and tried to open the windows.

Nope, too many coats of paint.

Belle gagged.

The spirits would arrive soon, and they needed to be ready. Both Sid and Belle searched the room as best they could, but nothing turned up, no dead rat, or opossum, no garbage or anything even more disgusting. As they searched for the source, however, the air cleared to a breathable state.

They lifted the chairs off the table, scooted it to the middle of the room, and placed a chair on one side of the table and the other two across from it. Sidra spread a midnight blue crushed velvet cloth on the table and Belle added three white candles and the offering of a bowl of rice.

It looked just the way the scene on the website looked when she researched the séance.

Something whizzed Sidra's head. She circled her arms overhead to drive away whatever dive-bombed. Her breath—but not her heart—was dead still.

I'm not taking another step, dear brother, until I see what that was; I don't care what you say.

She looked around, up and down, until she saw a small colony of bats settled upside down on beams overhead.

Breathing again, she refused to look at anything but the table set up under the lone light bulb, still uncertain whether or not spirits hid near where their bones had been discovered.

She slid a chair from the table, pulled matches from her pocket, and lit the three tall white candles in the center of the table. Flames flickered, making the bowl of rice look iridescent—glowing.

According to what Sidra read, to be successful, she needed to determine who she wanted to contact—or was that the leader's job?

Perhaps an ancestor, or whoever might be hanging out nearby. The latter frightened her.

Specific, Sidra, be specific.

So who? Miss Fancy—if that's the woman who visited her bedroom while she tried to sleep—if not, one of the other sisters. Miss Scarlet or Miss Lilly? If not them, then anyone who could offer guidance on what was going on in these houses. Hopefully, that was specific enough. To be more so would require her to know the information she sought from the séance.

Her heart felt like that of a tri-athlete on the last leg of a race. Pounded in her ears, stole her breath… The rapidity of the beat burned in her throat. She stopped, hands in her lap.

Breathe Sidra, breathe. In, out, in out, in out…trust the sisters, she told herself.

She cast a glance at Belle, who had taken a chair on the other side of the table. Then, wished she hadn't looked. Belle was no longer Belle—well, she was Belle, but she looked more like Margaret—resembling the painting of the women they'd seen downtown in the restaurant—and the woman Sidra saw behind her, reflected in the plate glass window.

There was no doubt, Belle—Margaret, was now in charge. She motioned to Sawyer, who, without any difficulty now, crossed the doorjamb and made his way to the table. He spoke not a word to either of them. With a quick questioning glance at Sidra and not even that to the woman in the other chair, he dropped like a dead weight into the third.

"Whew, we're really doing this." Belle, shivering, reached across the table and squeezed Sidra's hand. "You as jittery as I am?"

Sidra snorted. She wanted to ask Belle if she had any clue what she now looked like, but dared not. "I remember my brother telling me about one he'd sat in on, but it has been so long ago I don't recall any details. Anyway, here we are." She held her palms up.

"What do we do first?" Sawyer peered through his eyelashes. "We are supposed to decide who we want to contact. I've been thinking about it but want to hear from you two. This is your séance, not mine. I am the medium, at least I think that's what I'm called, to help assist you reach your ancestors—at least I guess that's who we're going for."

"What are your thoughts?" Belle tucked her hands in her lap.

"First one who came to mind is the figure who visits my room at night, crying. That or…"

"The women who sat in Miss Scarlet's living room in the middle of the night," Belle offered. "Or what about that old man I see outside who disappears so quickly?"

Sidra paused. At the moment, she'd go with anything Belle said. "Good idea. That reminds me of the old woman who calls me Miss White. Of course, she's not dead, but she does seem to disappear. She blows my mind. I have no connections with this town. I'm only here because of you."

Or are you?

"She's the only one you know here," Sawyer half choked out. "I don't know anyone. Damn, this is hard."

"Maybe we ought to just see who waits, ready to come, willing to…"

"That sounds okay, just don't know who we are opening the portal to—if such exists—and allow them in."

"Nothing ventured nothing gained; remember?" Belle scooted her chair in closer and reached for Sidra and Sawyer's hands.

As Sidra's eyesight adjusted to the darkness, she swore the air in the room shifted, altered the power. She breathed in a deep, cleansing breath, blinked and the room morphed into what she could only describe as a sepia-toned tintype photo. Old wood painted too many times, walls closing in, and the smell of dust rising from the floor.

The air hung still—stagnant.

"Okay," Sidra choked out, cleared her throat, and tried again. "Let's take several deep breaths and sit quietly for a moment."

She waited a minute, then lowered her voice and spoke. "Spirits from the past join us, move among us. Let the light of our candles represent the light of all that is holy and good in our world and visit us tonight. We brought gifts from life to offer and to connect life and death. Let our light be your light of the world."

The room grew quieter.

Faint, off in the distance, Sidra heard an ever so soft beat, then it stopped.

Started again.

Was she imagining it?

No, there it went again—like listening to her mother's heartbeat from inside the womb. She longed to look around her, but fear prevented movement.

Still, the beat remained, and went, and remained.

Other sounds began—sounds she wasn't sure she really heard.

Whispers—and then a hot breath blew down her collar.

She shivered.

A snap, a bump under the floor—like a waking nightmare about to happen, and then nothing.

Nothing but tension—everywhere, waiting, breathing, beating.

Sidra cleared her throat and called again, her voice cracking as she spoke. "Come! You who come from darkness to this place. SPEAK!"

The sound of shuffling feet swept across the dusty floor—entities from an unknown, unknowable place, bringing an unknown past and way too many kept secrets.

Quiet.

"Can't stand the silence," Sawyer whispered.

"Shh. Wait." Belle said.

A cold wind moaned around the corner of the house. Slider and Jenkins barked.

Couldn't be the moon, it wasn't out. Sidra's left hand

tingled like an electric current ran through it, and over to the right hand. She looked up. The other two appeared to be experiencing the same thing, and staring at their hands.

"Someone's here, or coming. Let's repeat the chant. Encourage them, help them feel safe."

They chanted then sat in silence.

"I'm here," a soft voice whispered, fearful—hesitant.

A force seemed to elevate Sidra's eyes from the candle flame to those of Belle and Sawyer, who both stared wide-eyed, drop-jawed, at Sidra.

Sidra gave them a questioning look then peeked around the room.

"Why are you here?" the voice asked. "Haven't we suffered enough? Why do you summon us from the dead?"

Sidra hiked her shoulders. Had they heard it? If so, from what direction did it come?

Belle squeezed Sidra's hand. "The voice is coming from…you… Sidra."

"Me? Is my mouth moving?"

"Not really, but—"

"Sawyer?"

"I agree with Belle. I don't see your mouth move, but your eyes sure change."

"Change? How?"

"Like—like, the color—like they belong to someone else—someone far away—like fire…"

Sidra snapped her eyes shut. Confused, yes, but mostly fearful.

"Tell me why you brought me here. What do you want?"

Belle looked at Sawyer and whispered, "I think we are supposed to ask yes or no questions, and since Sidra is the vessel from which we entered, it is up to you and me."

Sawyer shivered. "Okay, you first. I'm blank."

Belle cleared her throat. "Are you a woman or a man?"

"You must ask?" A deep, bass voice bellowed.

Sidra felt the leaders in her neck pulse as the voice spoke through her. Unable to respond, she pulled her energy inside and sat still—very still.

"Did you live in one of these houses?" Belle ventured a start.

"No."

"No? Hmmm. Okay."

"But you've been inside them?"

"Not inside, no."

"So outside?"

"Yesssss, I suppose you could say that."

"Did you know the family, the sisters?"

"You done gone meddling in things long past—dead and buried. Things best left buried."

"Too late for that," Sawyer said, "the sheriff's deputies already…"

"We know what they done—disturbed the dead, they did. And the dead ain't happy; I can tell ya that, and you three—you're playing with fire."

The voice sounded angry.

It held a tinge of—what? Regret? Sidra so wanted to jump in with questions she ached to ask. But the only part of her she held any control over was her thoughts.

The voice paused.

"Much evil here, don't you feel it?"

Belle looked at Sawyer, who looked at Sidra.

"Yes, we feel it," Belle said, staring straight into Sidra's eyes. "That's why we need your help."

"Ya need a heap more'n that, I tell ya fer shore. Cain't even hep me self. With that man in town ain't no body safe."

"What man?" Sawyer leaned in to Sidra.

"Yo daddy, that's who!"

"Whose daddy, mine?" Sawyer asked.

"Your'n and them gals—that's who ya need to yak at, not me, don't call me again, you hear?"

Whoosh!

Sidra's eyelids closed, her shoulders drooped, then nothing.

"Where'd he go?" The breathless voice of a young man yelled, like he'd been running through time—this side and that.

However, the words did not come from Sidra. The hoarse, angry words came from Sawyer. His eyes flashed, red, dark, threatening. "I said where'd he go? I've been chasing him forever, and now you let him go?"

Belle looked at Sidra, expecting her to do something it seemed. Hell's bells, do what? She shook her head at Belle, who glanced at Sawyer, or whoever had taken control of him.

"What's your name? Why are you here? Identify yourself." Belle said.

"No time. He's getting away again," the panicked voice said, fading off in the distance until only his breathing could be heard. At that point, Sidra didn't know who was in control. She did, however, know who wasn't—her.

After a few moments, Sidra opened her eyes to Belle and Sawyer staring at her like they'd literally seen the ghost they'd only heard—at least she thought that to be true.

The three agreed they had little choice but to continue, and indeed, that it may well be their last opportunity to learn what they came to learn.

Despite the most glaring dangers inherent in what they were about to undertake, they reminded each other that they controlled their own issues and whether or not they participated. However, they had no control over anyone or anything else.

Chapter Twenty-Nine
Miss Fancy

My petticoats swish as I pace the living room, not disturbing or misplacing a single dust mite, nor the trio in my path as I move through them and the pedestal table where they sit.

After several passes, I suck through my teeth and chin the group.

"These folks not so easy to run off like the others. Perhaps we've cut them short, my sweet sisters. Tourists, so-called ghost-hunters those looking for something—anything to excite their bored existence, they're easy to spook. These folks mean business. Next thing you know, they will beckon—summon us to join them. So do we, or do we not?"

"You're the eldest, Fancy. You tell us." A hint of derision tinges Scarlet's voice.

Lilly glares from me to Scarlet, the youngest—hence the most spoilt. "You two don't start that again. We're in this together, and we know the only way to be free is to deal with the past. The fact is, nothing else has ever freed us from this eternal hell."

"Perhaps that hawkshaw can," I say.

"Hawkshaw? You call that white-haired woman a hawkshaw?" Scarlet sneers. "You have no right to call another soul that—you with your uppity ways. For all you know, she may well be schooled at the one of the best."

"However," I say, blasting over the top of the other two arguments, "there is no way to control who comes through. I want freedom, yet I fear this might make matters worse. We are not certain that we have purchase on the truth, ourselves. Many charlatans have haunted us over the years. What if our effort makes things worse?"

"It cannot be worse, dear sister," Lilly says. "Hell is hell, and we have lingered in the midst of the flames for nigh a hundred years."

Scarlet struts to the red-velvet sofa, flounces down, and straightens her negligee. "*Well*," she humpfs, "you sound like you think it's all my fault we landed in the flames."

"Now, don't get your knickers in a knot. We know who's to blame, and it certainly isn't us," I say.

"What about this," Scarlet says as she moves to the edge of the sofa. "We each choose one of them to work with, hold their hands, so to speak, guide them through this danger-filled passage, thereby ensuring we escape at the end. If we fail, I fear we will not only stay trapped in this existence, but depending on who they might accidentally bring through or allow to escape, there may well be even more hell to pay."

"That makes sense, baby sister." I chuckle, surprised I paid Scarlet a compliment. Surely not the first one—I hope. "They might unintentionally call forth the dead without a clue who they want and who they don't want. Then we all suffer. We know the inherent danger because we remain in the midst of it yea these many years. What do you think, Lilly?"

"At this point, I do not see that we have much choice. Nothing yet has helped." Lilly pauses, staring at the three seated at the table. "Who takes which one?"

We observe those gathered around the table, who now sit in silence, unsure where to begin, or if to begin, each with varying expressions of fear and wonder—and doubt.

"Okay, we are all three in agreement," Lilly says. "We move forward. You know once we open the door— the door we have so carefully tended for more than a century, there is no such thing as going back."

"Let's proceed," I say. "As eldest, I choose the eldest—the hawkshaw." I flash Miss Scarlet's smirk right back at her. "My guess is she might well be the most stubborn."

Scarlet stares at the table's occupants, "I presume the youngest, Belle, they call her, is more of a kindred spirit to me than the other two."

Lilly chuckles. "You mean tends to be a mite rebellious?"

"Should you choose to use that word, smarty-pants."

"I choose." Lilly grinned. "Okay, that leaves the man they call Sawyer. I think I know who he is anyway—at least I have a sneaking suspicion."

"Who?" Scarlet and I ask in unison.

"Look at that nose, the wide-set eyes."

We stare at the man until Lilly will no longer tolerate our ignorance. "Acknowledge the corn, dear sisters. Deceive yourselves no more."

Frigid air blasts the front door wide. The house shudders and groans. Lights blink on and off, screams emanate from somewhere, then echo off in the distance until they turn into cold, cruel laughter.

We look at Lilly, our eyes stretched wide, our mouths open, and then both speak at the same time.

"Father?"

Chapter Thirty

A blast of warm air swirled around the room, and with it, a shift in energy. A softer, kinder air filled the room.

But it didn't last.

The hair on Sidra's arms raised.

"We didn't want to come," the words seemed to echo off the walls. "We begged not to, but we came, over and over and over."

"Who are you? What's your name?" Belle demanded. "Answer me, tell me the truth, or I won't let you stay. I will send you back to…"

"We mean you no harm. We are sisters, trapped within the walls of these houses for several lifetimes."

"What are your names?"

"You know our names."

"We know? How can we…oh, the doorplates." Belle

glanced from Sidra to Sawyer. Their expressions indicated they heard the same thing she did. She squeezed their hands.

Belle asked the question Sidra figured must be uppermost in her mind. "The woman in the painting at Margaret's Bar and Grill downtown. Who is she?"

"Madame Margaret."

The voices were indistinguishable, all melded together. The three spoke—if you could call it that—with one voice.

"Did you say Madam Margaret, as in bordello?" Belle sounded like someone punched her in the gut.

A high-pitched snicker echoed through the room.

"Were these houses…were you…prostitutes?"

"Women of the night, according to the Madame. Said we provided a service, but that was in a later lifetime."

Then a different voice spoke—if you could call it that. "Madame always claimed her patrons were perfect gentlemen. Indeed they should have been—she drew from the upper crust of society—doctors, lawyers, an Indian chief. Not to mention gangsters. The man they called the Arkansas Godfather—Owney Madden—spent his last thirty years in retirement right here in Hot Springs."

"Al Capone gave one of the girls syphilis—that's what killed her. Thank goodness the infant he sired didn't get it."

"Ruthless, vindictive, they were—all of them," came the whisper from the right rear corner of the room.

"How did that work for you?" Belle asked, her voice barely above a whisper.

Silence. Ugly, darkest black silence.

Until what seemed a singular entity communicated—not in words, but more…more…like thought to thought.

Sidra grab that pen and paper. This is important.

Whew! So Warren *was* here, after all. She followed his instructions.

"Ugly dark happenings—ugly dark—"

"Stop it, Fancy; stop it! That's in the past. It's…"

"It is NOT in the past." If ghosts can scream, this one sure did. Blood-curdling.

"You saw what happened. You saw what we women went through. Hell, literally. You went through it too—the abuse—although some had the audacity to call it fun. It is only fun if both people think so. I call it hell."

A younger voice chimed in. "Well, I liked the attention. I liked pleasing my customers. And Madame made sure the men protected us from—from…"

"You forgot your belly pain after Madam prepared that concoction for you to take."

"Yeah, but the same kind of concoction didn't work for her, did it?"

The room grew silent for what seemed a full ten minutes, but must have only been a second or two.

"The belly pain was easy—the hardest, most painful part, was staring at the bloody fluid staining the floor."

Voices, unidentifiable, but legion, came at them from all directions.

"Perhaps that is why we stay stuck here—"

"Oh, how soon you forget Papa."

"Which Papa?"

"You have to ask? You may be the youngest, but you weren't that young not to remember him—even though that was in a prior life for all three of us."

"Madam Margaret drove all the way to Dallas to see if a team of priests could come do an exorcism to rid these houses of his energy—ours too, I suppose. First thing the next week, they showed up. They wanted to bless the houses first—see if that worked. Madam closed the houses for a week, gave us all the week off, and left it to the priests.

"She went to Jefferson, Texas, where she ran another house, and spent the week there, then returned on Saturday. When she drove up, she found the priests piling into a carriage. They returned the money and hightailed it back to Dallas. No one ever knew what the priests saw, what they tried, and why it didn't work. But, business is business. A long line of customers stood out front waiting their turn."

"We knew. Haunts from prior lifetimes caused it."

The room grew eerily quiet in anticipation of someone or something—or dread of it.

"Where's the bastard?" A deep base voice interrupted a silence so thick even sunlight couldn't penetrate it. "Is he here? I demand to know where." The deep bass voice came from Sawyer, whose eyes rolled back in his head, and his jaw went slack.

"Identify yourself!" Belle said her voice as firm as it was loud. "Now, I said! If you fail to, you must leave. I command you."

"You command—huh!" Derision sounded in his words. "You ain't got nary control over me. Even those who tried ain't tried it for long. Nor lied to me neither! I can tell if you lie. I can see it in yourn eye. And then there's hell to pay. Ask Henry, he'll tell you."

"In all that is holy," Belle stood and pointed towards the door—like a door would make any difference. "Leave this house—and stay gone."

"Sweet cheeks, don't you worry your little head none. I demand you send that boy on his way. Don't let him stay. He's a troublemaker, pure and simple. Always has been, since the day he shoved his way out from between his ma's ugly fat thighs. Bad News Henry, I always called him."

The older male-sounding energy pulled away and settled in the shadows when a younger stronger voice interrupted. "Guess the means creates the ends—to them, at least. Ain't quite so with me. If I could have gotten to my sisters and Ma first—but knowing *the judge*, he would a butt in before I got a chance, anyway."

Startled at the speed of the switch, all emanating from Sawyer, Sidra glanced around when a cloud of bad breath filled the room, thick with the scent of cigarette smoke, stale beer, and old piss. "Belle," she whispered, "who's that?"

Nothing looked different—but the young male voice bouncing off the walls chilled her to the core. She pulled her sweater tighter.

The candles in the middle of the table flickered like someone puffed on them three times.

"I shouldn't never waited for my sisters," the young male continued. "As I recall, they would've been late to their own funeral. Not that we had one. This is what happens when you got the devil for a daddy."

Belle slammed her fist on the table. The candles vibrated and flickered once again. "I demand to know who you are—NOW!"

"Besides," the voice said, lower and deeper, "they don't look to be in a hurry to leave. I been waiting on them a long time. Think I'll go ahead on my own now."

"Go where?" Belle's voice rose. "You must identify yourself, or I will send you back into the blackness."

Chills coated chills, leaving Sidra regretting the idea of séance.

"I'm going, I'm going. But I'll tell you this. You're messing with danger—no, evil! My daddy wrote the book on it. Satan himself took lessons."

Sawyer slumped, his chin dropping to his chest. All color drained from his face. Silence, deeper than any Sidra ever experienced, fell on them.

Now what do we do, sweet Warren?

Hang on. You're just getting started.

"Miss White? Miss White?" The quivering voice of an elderly woman whispered over Sidra's shoulder. She leapt out of her chair, and it banged on the floor. "Did you hear that?" She asked the others.

"Hear what?"

"Oh, no. Don't tell me I'm the only one who heard it." She grabbed the chair, righted it, and stared around the room. "Someone just whispered in my ear, calling me Miss White. You mean neither of you heard it?"

Belle and Sawyer shrugged, with no idea what she meant.

"I'm telling you, someone called me Miss White."

"Well, did you answer?" Sawyer gave a nervous laugh. "Maybe you should."

"Sure, either answer or accept the fact I'm going crazy." She steadied the chair and sat. "Okay, whoever you are, you know my name, but I don't know yours. If you want to talk to me, you need to introduce yourself. Otherwise, I demand you leave us be."

The room grew quiet while Sidra let the entity consider her words, only paying attention to her own breath—in, out, in out. Losing track of time. She remained still, breathing deeply, eyes closed. Belle and Sawyer made not a sound. Even their breathing sounded slow, silent almost.

The quivery-sounding voice of an old woman came at them from all directions. "You need not fear me. I intend you nor your friends no harm. A bright white light surrounds each of you. That tells me you stand for all that is good. Lord knows these girls need that. Lifetime after lifetime, they have paid for crimes not of their making— and pay still, today. I beg you, free them from this hell. They deserve none of it."

"Who are you? Name, please?"

"Sophia, the sister of Esther—the mother of the girls—and the eldest, a boy named Henry, though I barely knew him. His days here came much later than their arrival. Too late—I'd say. He tried, but…" The voice grew weak and stopped for a full thirty seconds or more before it continued.

"You see," the voice explained, "I lived here before they came—Esther and her girls—and him."

"Him, as in the son?" Sidra's breathing had settled closer to normal, but her mind raced like a forest fire.

"No, not the son—the Judge, Esther's husband, and the children's father. I use the term father quite loosely."

"Go on."

"It's a long story."

"And how does Miss White fit into it, and why did you call me that?"

"You want that story first or last?"

"Do they fit together?"

"Yes, ma'am, they do—matter of fact, they all do, somewhere down the line."

Sidra cleared her throat, the thought of holding her breath entered her mind, but she figured the story might be too long for that. She caught a quick glimpse of Belle and Sawyer. Their eyes had grown foggy—like they'd gone somewhere else and left Sidra alone.

Good lord, what were they getting into?

"Then give it to us first." Sidra's voice croaked.

The story continued, but the process changed. Sidra felt the story rather than heard it. She saw a young girl who reminded Sidra of her own daughter. The girl sat with her mother on what looked like the front row pew of a church. The man at the pulpit was her father. He preached hellfire and brimstone—his face fire red, his cheeks puffed. Soon, the service ended. The girl's mother took her hand, saying, "Come on, Mary, we have to get home and get Sunday dinner on the table."

They scooted out the side door while the congregation filed out front, stopping to shake her father's hand in the vestibule. "Preacher White, you always tell us how the cow ate the cabbage. You made my toes bleed, you stomped on them so much." The man behind the speaker said, "Yep, the preacher's gone from preaching to meddling." The folks grouped around the preacher laughing, agreeing—and idolizing the man. Her father...

Next, Mary, older now, stood beside her mother, watching a house fire rage like an inferno.

"That's enough for now," Sophia's voice blasted in

the room. Folks can only handle so much at one time."

"Is that girl me?"

"Nah, she ain't."

Sidra let out a deep sigh.

"But she's your ancestor."

"My…? My family isn't from Arkansas."

"Your mama's family shore was."

"By the name of White?"

"Yes'm."

Sidra had not expected to learn about her own past while working on Belle's case. This was Belle's family. Surely the old hag did not know what she was talking about. Time to move on to another subject…the fire.

Chapter Thirty-One

The old hag settled into a steady stream of storytelling—yet, again, it wasn't telling, like using words, it seemed more like scenes flashed behind Sidra's eyes.

Is it the same for Belle and Sawyer, she wondered, but didn't dare open her eyes to check.

Images unfolded before her. Images of a crusty man in a full black beard, a long split-tail black coat over a white shirt topping black pants. He hunkered over what looked to be a rough sketch of houses for the three sisters. She sensed the old man did not want the girls living in his house with him and their mother. Even after completion, however, their mother lived with the daughters, and not the father, which sent him into a fiery rage.

The scene flash forwarded to the same man, still in black, sitting on the bench in a rustic courtroom, holding a wooden gavel in his right hand, and pounding the bench. Fury raged in his eyes. "He's guilty," he yelled at the policeman accompanying the accused. "If you had any sense you'd see that. Look at his eyes! It's obvious the man's guilty. Put him in the holding cell."

Again, the scene changed, revealing small groups of people gathered downtown, in bars, in churches, on street corners, whispering, fearful, unsure, checking over their shoulders to see who might overhear. Sidra concentrated on the few scattered words she caught here and there.

Two hundred now, the man in the faded green shirt whispered. *More than that*, another corrected. *What's he doing with them?* A frightened red-haired boy asked, pulling on the shirttail of another. *It's murder, I tell you! Someone's got to stop him. He's crazy in the head!*

Scenes flashed forward like someone pulled them across a computer screen. A backyard—someone's backyard—a familiar backyard.

The backyard behind *this* house—the *sister* houses.

The large oak tree, only much smaller, a noose looped over a large branch, a man swinging from the rope by the neck, his legs kicking, jerking, slowing.

As fast, the scene changed again, this time, it moved downtown, a group of people looked for something—or someone. They shuffled off, their pace increasing the further they went, heading down through the middle of town, up the hill towards three white, narrow, Victorian-style homes. They climbed the hill, passed the three homes to a fourth house on the other side. Someone banged on the front door.

No response.

Another man stepped up and yelled something she couldn't quite grasp, yet the intent grew clearer. Whoever lived in that house–their presence was requested. Now!

Still no response.

The tall skinny man in the rear broke away from the group and ran behind the houses.

"He's back here! Hurry!"

In the backyard, the judge stood over a young man tied to a tree, yelling, "Help! For the love of God, somebody help me! He's a crazy."

A man at the rear of the group yelled, "I'm gettin' the sheriff! Don't let him get away."

Startled by a sudden flash, and fire in her face, Sidra shoved her chair back, panic rising in her throat, choking on fumes and flaming wood.

Where was she? How did she get here? Where were Belle and Sawyer?

Someone screamed, "Sidra, Sidra, it's okay. We're here. What is it?"

"Fire—house on fire," she choked out. "We've got to get out," she fought the tight grip on her arms. "Don't you see it? Smell it? Taste it?"

Someone held both her arms, shaking her, pushing a glass of water to her lips. A far-off voice called her name, begging her to come back…but who was it? What did they want with her?

"Don't you see the greedy flames, the exploding embers? Why can't you…see it? There, see that little girl? Over there! Look! See me burying my face in my mother's apron? That's me, isn't it? It looks like me, but…"

"But you didn't live that long ago," a familiar voice whispered in her ear.

Ice-cold water splashed her face. Belle and Sawyer came into view. Flames receded behind them, along with the noises befitting a horse and buggy loaded with something evil. Eyes glared from the inner darkness.

Her chest pounded, sweat coated her armpits. "Evil, something…oh my gosh, let me sit down, catch my breath." Hands shaking, she stumbled to her chair, trying to catch her breath.

The smell of smoke faded, only to be replaced by a sense of frigid air around her feet. She jumped up, looked under the table. Nothing.

"Did you see it?" she asked.

"See what," Belle and Sawyer both asked at the same time.

"The house burning—me standing in the front yard—but wait, no, she said it wasn't me, because I didn't live that long ago."

"She?" Belle clasped Sidra's hands.

Sidra looked around the room but saw no one, heard nothing.

"Sophia, I guess. I used to know a Sophia. Rented a room from her—upstairs, over her old two-story home."

"When was that?" Sawyer leaned forward and rested his hand on top of Belle's on top of Sidra's.

"Not long ago. A year or so, right after I moved to Orange and took over The Third Eye. It was wintertime, too, right after I found Slider." She grew quiet, remembering, then, "Sophia was a mystic. Something about her leads me to think—no, not the same person, but related." She shook her head. "This is weird, too weird. I really never believed in this kind of stuff."

Oh, yes, you did, baby sister. Oh, yes, you did.
Warren?

Sawyer cleared his throat and said, "Was it the house next door that burned? The one you saw?"

"I think, yes. It must have been."

Sidra went on to recount the fire scene, the buggy, and the evil.

Belle pulled her jacket tighter. "I think we are getting close, sweetheart. Are you okay? We must protect ourselves in this, and I sense you were getting sucked into the fire."

"Not the fire so much, as the memory of it." She paused, aware something niggled at the edge of the memory. Someone calling. Her? No, her mother—at least the girl that looked like her mother. They called her White. Mrs. White. *Oh good lord, Warren, was that us? Where were you?*

Gone to get the sheriff, I think.

But how could we be so…so connected to…

People move, baby sister, even then. You remember our family has always tended to have wanderlust. Plus, if I'm right, one of our ancestors got run out of town—folks called her a witch. Said she cast spells. Really, I think all she did was convince people to bathe in the hot mineral springs and tap into healing power of the crystal veins running underneath this area.

Oh, good lord. She couldn't share that with anyone.

Or could she?

"Okay, you saw a house fire?" Belle scooted her chair closer to the table. "The judge run out of town, a man tied to the tree in the back yard saved…what else?"

Sidra shrugged. "That's basically it—at least I think it is. But that doesn't explain all the bones buried under the house."

"It does if that's where the judge buried all those he killed." Sawyer mused.

"True. The judge swore he could tell whether a man was guilty by looking in his eyes. He became not only judge, but also jury and executioner. The townspeople grew suspicious after so many that were arrested flat dropped out of sight. One day a crowd marched up the hill only to find the judge beating a prisoner to death behind the sister's houses. They ran him out of town and that night set fire to his house, next door. No one ever saw him, his wife, or his daughters again."

"How do you know that?"

"I'm not sure," Sidra said, "but afterward is when the sister's houses were said to be haunted. Thing is, I don't recall seeing the sisters, or the mother, in the buggy on the way out of town. Just evil."

Chapter Thirty-Two

Sidra lost all sense of how she knew what she knew, or even if she knew. Had Warren somehow fed her information without her knowing it?

Niggling goosebumps chilled her. She shivered and drew her sweater tighter...until goosebumps became—became...

A contraction?

She'd experience childbirth and the pain that entailed, and for the life of her, this vice around her midsection felt similar. Panicked, she shot a glance at Belle and Sawyer, who were fading into nothingness. She clawed at her swollen belly, as the pains grew stronger, hoping for comfort, trying to pull back from the growing pain, but found only more. Her fingers ripped at the crumpled, wet quilt underneath her as the pains grew into one gigantic, never-ending push in search for release.

"She's getting close," a voice said. "I see the head. Poor thing, if she'd—"

"She waited too long," a muffled voice from the other side whispered.

Didn't they know? Didn't they know she had no other choice? That she…that she… A burst of pain slashed everything else away, all thought, all regret, all questions, all sorrow, all shame.

It all flooded back in the whimper of a newborn.

Then mercifully, nothing.

"Is she okay? What's happening?"

"I have no idea. Sid, Sid… Are you okay? What's going on? Talk to us."

A hand shook her, gently at first, then with more urgency. "I think so, yes. Why?" Sidra straightened from a slump and saw Belle hovering over her.

"Why? Because you were acting crazy…talking out of your head…about some baby or something." Sawyer spoke from across the table.

"I don't know what happened—like I knew it was me…but it wasn't me. Like I watched…watched—no, felt—someone having a baby. I heard it cry—damn it, I felt the pain. Like it was me—but it wasn't me." She glanced at her quivering hands and rested them in her lap. "That's crazy sounding…"

"Maybe we should call a halt to this." Concern coated Sawyer's voice.

"No way in hell you're stopping this now." A strange voice shouted from the rear corner of the room.

Another voice, weaker, hoarse, added to the din. "You got all this going. You can't quit now. You owe it to us to see this through."

Sidra, Sawyer, and Belle looked at each other then in

the direction of the voices, each distinct, with varying pitch and degrees of strength, yet each urgent, demanding.

Added to that, the overpowering smells of cigarette smoke and body odor.

"Just 'cause you cain't see us, don't mean we ain't here." A younger, intense voice came from near the front door.

Good God, were they surrounded?

"Fact is—we been here long time—even before them painted ladies having babies they should've never had."

"You mean Miss Scarlet, Miss Lilly, and Miss Fancy?" Belle spoke in the general direction of the last voice.

"Nah, not them!" Several voices spoke up. "They's victims just like us." Irritation coated the words—but Sidra lost count of which voice, from where. They all seemed to meld into one giant, overpowering presence.

Who are you?" Belle asked. "We can't help you if we don't know who you are."

"Makes no difference our names. We's those souls the judge-jury-executioner kilt. Didn't matter to him none whether we done what he said or not. We looked guilty, we was guilty."

The voice, or voices, seemed both reluctant, and at the same time, eager to talk.

"Some of us done it, some of us ain't, but all of us got buried in the basement anyway. We tired being trapped here with them sisters. They tired, too. We all ready to go on to our just rewards. Flames a hell cain't be much worse."

"He left his daughters here?" Belle's words caught in her throat. "Why are their souls trapped? Didn't they go with him and his wife?"

"Yeah, well, some of them bones ain't ours."

"Huh!" A youngish-sounding voice chimed in. "I can tell you why. Same reason—they daddy killed them, too, shotgun blast mowed 'em down when they said they ain't going and he said they not staying. Took a shotgun to 'em, the missus screaming all the while. He shot her too, and hightailed it outta town."

"Sins of the father," Sawyer said. "We heard the judge had a son, too. What happened to him?"

"Got off the train just in time to see town folk torch his old man's house. Them flames reached the high heavens."

Confusion crossed Belle's face. "What about babies. Sidra here…"

"Don't need to walk them hogs any further, I tell you that. Folks couldn't live in them houses after that 'cause them sister's never left. They walk them floors even now, trapped.

"When them gangsters came in after the big war, a madam bought the land and houses real cheap and opened for business. She ain't had no problem getting customers—between the sheriff and the mayor, Capone, Madden, and them others, she got rich. Thing is, them babies had a way of coming whether they's wanted or not—many a seed was planted with nary a harvest, if you git my drift."

A second male voice interrupted. "Well, that ain't perzactly the whole story. Margaret's' baby made it through—even though her mama tried to stop it—but she waited too late. Named her Beulah. Poor mite was so tiny they didn't think she'd make it—she made it all right and ended up inheriting the property."

Belle's mouth dropped open. "Beulah? That's the name Maxx showed me on the title Mother kept locked away in the safe."

"Now, if you're done with us, can you say a prayer or something and let us be on our way? A few years back, when that Madam got some priests to come rid the houses of our kind, we should've behaved nicer. Those guys were scared of their own shadow."

A snicker came from further back. Then a chorus of

laughter filled the corner. "Yeah, if we'd a knowed we'd be trapped here, we'd a behaved nicer to them white robe guys with rosaries. You should've seen them skedaddle."

"That's what we git for you not listening to me." Sidra heard the words coming out of her mouth, yet knew they were not hers. "We could've been gone long ago, but no, some of you wanted to hang around here to take care of the three sisters—felt sorry for them, did ya? Well, now we're stuck here for sure—less these folks can help."

"You need...our...help?" Sidra felt Belle's eyes focused on her mouth, never venturing up to her eyes, which was bound to be full of questions.

"Ask how we can help, Belle. What can we do to free these entities," Sawyer said.

"Ain't nobody ever tried to help us before. When we show up, they run like scared rabbits. Never seen folks disappear so fast."

"Ask, Belle, ask!" Sawyer's urging grew stronger.

Belle's gaze rose to Sidra's, and the instant she did, Sidra felt the entities leave. And as they left, so did the flame in the candles.

"They've gone," she said.

The three sat in stunned silence, letting the energy that had consumed them disseminate. Sidra looked at her watch. The hour felt like days.

The air cooled once again. Sidra glanced at Sawyer, who sat in stunned silence. "You okay," she asked.

He nodded. "I think I am," he said in a half-whisper. "I never would have believed I'd experience what we sat through. Never believed in entities before—that kind, at least."

"And now?" Sidra smiled.

"No denying...did you two hear and see the same thing I did? It's obvious souls have been trapped here for generations. Did I hear right? They asked us to help? How do we do that?"

"One thing I heard is that all those who the judge

killed and buried the bodies under the house, their souls are trapped here."

"Also, the spirit of those fetuses buried under the house…blows my mind, I don't…" Belle, said.

Sidra glanced out the window as the sun peeped over the horizon. "I don't know about you, but I think I've handled about all I can for one night. Let's go get some sleep."

They trudged across the lawn to Fancy.

Both dogs met them at the front door, tails between their legs. Like Sidra felt.

Once inside, she and Slider headed straight to bed. Slider turned in circles, then settled beside her and fell in a deep sleep. She lay wondering how to cleanse spirits from the houses, not just spirits, but many spirits, too many to count.

She settled her breathing and closed her eyes to Andrine Gilbeaux, smiling. Her beautiful white teeth glistened in bright sunlight, and her coal-black hair hung in ringlets. The psychic lived in the middle of Blue Elbow Swamp, the backwaters of the Sabine and Neches rivers between Texas and Louisiana. Sidra held vivid recall of her first visit to Andrine's, traveling in a small pirogue paddled by a toothless old man. She and her first client braved the journey to see if Andrine could help her client connect with a dead woman.

She had.

Sidra's first and lasting impression was the woman's loose-fitting outfit and long strings of beads. Her ebony, wrinkled skin glistened. Something about the woman drew Sid into her warm, soft, and gentle arms. She felt the same way now.

"Andrine," Sidra said, whether in her head or into the room, she knew not. Nor did she care. "I'm glad to see you. I need your help."

Den I come at de right time. I tho't I heard you calling last night. Wha'cha need, honey chile?

"I need to know how to clear a house of entities."

Good ones, or bad ones?

"I'm not sure—I think mostly good, but a lot of bad, too. The first ones got trapped in these houses due to the sins of an evil man, actually their father."

You seen dem?

"And how! They all showed up last night, begging us to find a way to release them. I was nervous enough trying to conduct séance—I sure don't want to screw up releasing them from this hell they've endured for over a hundred years, and I'm not sure what a ghost is. You know my past, Andrine… I never—"

Well, I reckon you know as much as the next preacher's wife. She hooted at her own joke, then caught her breath and settled into explaining.

A ghost is a disembodied person who, for some reason or the other, has trouble going into spirit world. Sometimes they don't know how to move on or are scared to go. Some stay behind to finish something they left unfinished. They show up maybe like mist or orbs of light. They take up a lot of energy when they do, that's why people talk about cold spots.

Sidra tried to absorb it all while her head spun. She shifted and eased under the blankets, sorry now she'd ever taken this job. Murders she could solve. Murderers she could catch. What on earth made her think she could handle spirits, left behind energies of an unknown past?

Somethin' else… Wait, something ain't right. There's more here than you think.

"What? I don't understand?" Sidra racked her brain for missing pieces. She knew the judge killed over two hundred men simply because he decided they were guilty, whether they were or not. Then killed his daughters and his wife when they refused to leave when he got found out. He had a son named Henry, who arrived too late to help.

What was Sidra missing? Yes, the houses had become brothels, and yes, one might accurately guess that pregnancies started, and many ended behind these walls. But what else might she have missed?

It's got to do with you, Sid. Where do you come in?

"I'm assisting Belle…and Sawyer, too, it seems. When we started, we had no idea he was connected to this story, but…"

You too smart to think that, Ms. Smart. You know if the three of you done gone there to uncover the truth, every one of you has some truth to uncover about ye self, or ye past, or ye—

"I'm a believer now, for sure."

Yeah, let me git me cards and pull one for ye.

Sidra knew what cards Andrine meant. Tarot. All her life, Sidra doubted the foolishness of such nonsense— however, after meeting Andrine and her working with Sidra and her first client, she no longer doubted anything Andrine said.

Ye there? Hold on…

In her mind, Sidra heard cards shuffling, and the light breath of her weird friend.

Here it is. This what you was needing? Someone from your past—White, white—either she always wore white or her name was…she…well, she… That's what you got to follow up on Sid. Find her. Ask her what she meant. Who she know, why she call you that?

Oh good lord. This wasn't what Sid wanted to hear. She could help Belle all day long, but she had no intention of working on any of her own past. She'd already done that. At least she thought she had.

"But the entities here already told me about all that. Do I have to talk to her personally?"

Don't have to do nothing. Andrine chuckled. *You called and asked. I tell you what I sees. It's up to you what you want to do about it.*

I don't care what you do with candles and crosses and salt. Not even sure those things work—at least like people like to think they do. Yer way to the other side of this situation is through. No short cuts. Andrine's words were short, clipped, then she grew quiet, waiting…

Sid knew her well enough to know she wasn't done yet.

Youse only six degrees separated from that Miss Belle, and Sawyer guy.

"I know. The spirits said—"

Youse? A Yankee Bayou witch. I mean it's no coincidence that you three are there together. Youse as connected to the past of them houses as them other two.

Sidra tried to clear her head, but too many thoughts lay piled on top of each other.

Ye there?

"Yes, I'm here. I guess I'm more confused than ever. I don't…"

Then find that old woman.

Damn.

Chapter Thirty-Three

Belle stuck her head around the door. "You okay? I thought I heard you talking…" She glanced around Sidra's bedroom as though she expected to see someone else.

Startled, Sidra sat up and swung her legs to the side of the bed. "I'm fine." She laughed. "Must have been dreaming. Didn't know I was talking in my sleep."

"Well, if you were dreaming then you slept more than me. Afraid the longer I lay in bed the more my mind races. What's next?"

Delaying Andrine's advice, Sidra decided to cover all her options. "I need to go to town and pick up a few things, then, when I get back, let's see what we can do to free these trapped souls."

Sidra remembered seeing a shop on Central Avenue called The Metaphysical Connection and headed there. After explaining the task ahead of her, the knowledgeable clerk collected a series of items and explained their use in house clearing.

Sidra made her purchase and came home with bundles of dried sage, a shell, box of matches, a turkey feather, and a box of sea salt, plus a bottle of Hot Springs mineral water.

They spent the afternoon smudging, burning sage bundles, and clearing each house of negative energies. To cover all their bases, they followed the guidance of the woman who sold Sidra the items and sprinkled sea salt along the window ledges and the door jams.

Next, they asked the unwanted spirits to leave. "Your time here is gone. You don't belong here anymore. It is time for you to move on. We release you of any leftover issues, problems, wounds."

"We wish you well in your new place and order you to leave this property now. You need to move on."

A sudden whoosh felt like it pulled all the energy from the house. Screams of metamorphic pain, pain of release, of healing, of celebration grew so loud, Sidra, Belle, and Sawyer held their ears.

The sound of rushing water soon turned into a whirlwind of rushing air, moving to the ceiling, circling the room, and finally out the roof. In the distance, Sidra heard what she could only describe as girls giggling. Their departure drained the air from the room. Sidra struggled to catch her breath. The other two also labored to breathe. The lights flickered a couple of times, then glowed brightly.

After the longest, quietest time, Sawyer glanced around then back to Sidra and Belle. "You think that's it? You think they left?"

Don't trust it, Sis. Spirits can fool you. Time will tell.

"Maybe. Maybe not." Sidra stretched and twisted at the waist a couple of times. "Time will tell."

Chapter Thirty-Four

Over the next few days, a peace settled over the houses. No spirits or ghosts showed themselves. Sidra, Belle, and Sawyer agreed the air they breathed felt fresher, cleaner. Even Slider and Jenkins seemed at peace.

One morning, Sawyer brought up the *what's next* topic. "Think you might be able to put these houses on the market now?"

"I don't see why not." Belle paced the room. "Maybe we need to talk to that realty and see what they think."

Irritated when Andrine's admonishment came to mind, Sidra attempted to shove the words to the back of her thoughts.

The persistent old woman refused to go.

Warren was another matter.

You not going to ignore Andrine, are you?

I can't deal with this at the moment, Warren."

Then get to where you can, 'cause I'm not going anywhere until you do.

"Excuse me a couple of minutes," she told the others. "I'll be right back," and headed to her bedroom.

Ignore? And how in the world do you know Andrine, much less what she said?

I know most anybody I want to, sweet Sis. Thing is, I also know that old crone who called you Miss White. I know what she meant by calling you such. One of those secrets I kept from you—for your own good, of course.

Frustration and reluctance raged inside Sidra's gut as she flopped in the rocking chair in the corner of her room

Get up and go do it!

All right, Warren, all right, damn it. I'll go.

She pulled on a jacket and warm shoes, told Belle and Sawyer of her need for fresh air, and trudged down the hill in the general direction of where she assumed the old crone lived.

After a few minutes walk down an unpaved path, she noticed an old shack tucked way back in a corner lot overgrown with shrubs, weeds and brush. A small stovepipe stuck out a clouded window, whiffs of smoke trialing overhead.

Sidra stepped carefully, shoving aside dead branches, rocks, and general trash, rusted cans, empty bottles.

She rapped on the rough-hewn door.

She rapped again. On the other side, muffled footsteps shuffled her way.

Sidra held her breath, trying to decide whether to run or stay—or hide behind a bush.

The door creaked open.

The old crone stood holding the handle. She looked unsure whether to open the door any further. She took one look at her visitor, tightened a drab wool scarf reeking of Vick's Vapor Rub and opened the door wider. "Been waitin' for you. Come on in outta the cold." The crone opened the door enough for Sidra to pass.

Inside the dark, damp, musty room a fire raged in a blackened wood stove. The stove, and what little furniture filled the room came from another era. A narrow door in the rear must lead to a toilet, Sidra guessed. A single bed with a threadbare chenille bedspread sat shoved up against the wall to her right. A rocking chair next to it still rocked a little, as if the crone got up to answer the door. A small kitchen counter on the other side supported an old sink, a couple of battered granite dishpans, and a few odd and end utensils and dishes. A large rag rug covered the middle of the gray plank floor. One small window let in the little light available. The crone walked over to a small lamp and clicked it on. "I don't need much light," she said. Can't see with it or without it."

Sidra cleared her throat. "I hope I haven't interrupted you."

"Not much to interrupt." She hacked.

"I suppose you know why I'm here."

"Been waitin'."

"That first day we met you called me Miss White."

"That's your name—leastwise your great grandma's.

"I never knew I had family from Arkansas."

"Well, I reckon that's 'cause Miss White, the girl that borned your great grandmama died, and her family gave her away."

"I don't understand." Confusion covered Sidra like a holocaust cloak.

The old crone backed up to the woodstove and lifted her long skirts, exposing her backside to the heat. "These old bones don't handle the cold anymore."

The room grew quiet, except for the occasional crackle of the fire and a rattle in the old crone's chest every time she inhaled.

Sidra worried about the old crone burning herself on the stove and started to warn her, but the set jaw advised otherwise.

"So my grandmother was illegitimate?"

"A bastard, that's what they called the child in them days."

"How do you know all of this?" Sidra asked.

"I don't tell all my secrets."

"So Miss White had a girl?"

"That she did. Prettiest baby you ever did see. Pink skin, black hair and blue eyes. A real beauty."

"So what happened?"

"Town gossip went wild, but your great grandma faced it all down, loved and cared for that baby like no bodies' business. Never said who the daddy was. My mama had her suspicions, but she wouldn't tell. Anyway, a few months later, your great grandma died of syphilis, and then the baby disappeared. Folks said her family gave the baby away."

Sidra pushed. "So did your mama ever learn the father?"

"Yes ma'am. She knowed. Never would tell a soul—'cepting me after I guessed right."

"Who?"

"It was one of them mob guys down from Chicago. Hear tell, the fourth floor of the Arlington Hotel belonged to him, at least when he was in town. You talk about haunted! That place has all kinds of ghost stories about it."

"The hotel downtown across from the fountain?"

"One and the same. My niece used to work there—what did they call her—oh yes, a desk clerk. She had the night shift. Said one night—or early morning, if I recollect, she was all alone at the front desk when a picture frame fell over all on its own, seems like. She got up to go right it when the jacket she'd rested on the back of her chair, flew up real high then slammed down on the floor. Said she had to sign a piece of paper saying she'd never tell anyone about any ghosts at the hotel, but after she quit, she shore did!"

"Who was the ghost?" Sidra questioned, wondering if

it were the house sisters.

"Ain't sure, but I swear it be the baby's father."

"Who? Please tell me."

"Capone was his name, Al Capone. Gave syphilis to your great grandma, he did. Course them days they didn't have no medicine to treat it 'cept them mercury baths down at the baths. Here tell they still have the bathtub where they dunked him. Didn't do no good though. Takes more'n mercury to kill that stuff."

"What happened?"

"Miss White's mama kept the baby long as she could. Then a sister who lived in Texas came in on a train and got the child. Last I heard, she raised that baby as her own."

Sidra wondered if Warren knew all that history. If he had, why hadn't he told her?"

The room grew quiet while Sidra tried to imagine what life must have been like for her great grandmother.

Miss White. Hmmm, well, I'll be damned. Mama told me that story years ago, but I never believed her. She always was one to stretch the truth—that's why I never told you.

Warren! So you did know.

Chapter Thirty-Five

Sidra's head felt trapped by concentric circles by the time the late evening sky began to darken. Wind whistled around her as she made her way back up the hill. She reached for the hood on her jacket and realized she'd left the clothing at the old woman's house. She did a one eighty and hustled down the hill.

Following the same path she'd taken earlier, when she reached the location where the old shack had been, she stopped dead in her tracks. The lot was empty. No shack, no old crone, nothing except the Vick's Vapor Rub-soaked woolen scarf the old woman wore tied around her neck, now in a heap on the ground. Trash littered the area. At the rear of the lot, she saw rows of rusty barbed wire manacled to a rotten fence post—and her burnt-red jacket, flapping in the wind.

No woodstove pipe protruded from any window, no

smoke spiraled into the ethers, no weathered wood—no shack, no crone, none of the musty smells, only an askew fence post and Sidra's trapped jacket.

Her feet felt glued to the earth. Unable to blink, much less flee, she stared at the jacket until a cold wet nose nudged her hand.

"Slider? How long have you been standing there?" She submerged both hands into his thick red fur, thankful something felt solid and warm. "I think I'm going crazy." Her voice quivered. "I could have sworn a house sat here a few minutes ago. Did you see it?"

Whining, Slider ducked his head, curled his tail between his legs and barked at the flapping jacket.

"Okay, let's get out of here." She dashed to the barbed wire, freed the captive jacket, and the two fled up the hill.

If only such action freed her from the storm of questions clouding her mind.

After a light dinner, the three of them and the dogs huddled around the fireplace chatting. Sawyer prepared hot chocolate. Their shared experiences the past few days seemed to have bonded the relationship between he and Belle into more good friends than anything else. That felt good to Sidra. Belle could always use friends who knew and accepted her.

Events of the day—of Sidra's day—did not get relayed. Instead, Sidra harbored them in her thoughts—at least for now. Maybe tomorrow she'd share them with the others, but since her life—the history of her ancestors, had no impact on theirs, she convinced herself she did not have to reveal the information from the old crone.

Exhausted, and needing time to think about the day, Sidra excused herself early, leaving Slider curled up in front of the fireplace. She crawled into bed with the words of the crone resonating in her thoughts. Only then did she realize she'd never even learned the woman's name.

Had her biological great grandmother really provided *services* for the likes of Al Capone? Died as a result of such? How much of this did her parents know? They'd both died when Sidra and Warren were both fairly young—plus, her mother never had been one to reveal personal issues.

But Al Capone? Good grief. Holy cow!

So she and Warren both had gangster genes in their DNA. Was that why Warren loved catching the bad guys? Was that why he insisted she inherit his business—to keep *getting* the bad guys? To reverse any criminal influence that flowed in their blood?

White, White. Something about the name rang a bell from so long ago Sidra could not wrap her memory around it.

Where are you Warren? Warren? Damn it! Did you know all this? She flipped from her left, to her right side, to flopping over on her stomach, then on her back, thinking, thinking, questioning—but nothing made sense. Not anymore.

Then, again, what difference did it make? That was all in the past. Not a part of her life today. With that, she allowed her thoughts to drift until something caused her to sit straight up in bed, heart pounding. She scanned the room. Had someone come in?

Nothing looked out of place. Must be her out-of-control imagination again. After all, the last few hours gave reason for anyone's imagination to run rampant. Restless, she swung her legs off the bed, padded to the window and instantly slammed her hand over her mouth to squash a scream.

Silhouetted against a lowing hanging moon, a male figure, decked out in a loose-fitting black suit, leaned against the balcony railing.

Who was it, and even more, what the hell did he

want?

He didn't appear to have seen her at the window. She stepped further into the darkness to observe him without exposing her presence.

A white fedora with a black band looked sat thumbed to the back of the man's head. One hand rested, tucked in his coat pocket, while the other held a big glowing cigar, the smoke disappearing into the air without leaving a single clue behind, including a smell. He'd crossed his legs at the ankles like he had nowhere to go and all night to get there. His shoes were black too, except for the slashes of white on the sides.

Spectators?

Questions flooded her brain as her knees turned to rubber and a flashing bright light blinded her. She staggered to the bed, head reeling.

"So, what game you playing me for?"

Sidra heard the words, yet she'd swear the man's mouth hadn't moved. Instead, as crazy as it seemed, his words—thoughts maybe—seemed imbedded in the route of smoke as it left his mind and exited his mouth.

Al Capone leapt into her thoughts without bidding.

"Don't take the verbiage *game* wrong. I'm talking 'bout all the goings-on in these houses stirring up a past that's best left dead and buried. Some folk don't know how to leave the past be."

"Are you for real?" Sidra felt stupid asking the question to a man long dead, but who now sat in the rocking chair across from her bed.

"Don't try playing games with me, doll. I'm already on the other side, and I've learned a lot more since I been here. You folks living today take things too literal, too seriously."

"Not sure what you mean by that."

"Ain't much on formality, but, look kid, you could've done much worse for a relative."

"Excuse me?"

"Look how long it took you to get out of that first game."

"Game?"

"Playing like the perfect preacher's wife. Hell, only thing important to him was his own ego and martyrdom. Total lack of self-awareness. Tried to tell you that before you married him, but no…you wouldn't listen.

"Folks judge me for all the men I killed—never killed any what didn't need killing." He paused, lifted the cigar to his mouth and inhaled. On exhale the smoke appeared as an embodiment of the souls of those he'd killed. He gave a one-sided grin as though he liked seeing them disappear in front of his eyes again. Guess he hadn't made much progress on that part of his history.

"You just don't screw over people. Thing is, many of them self-righteous preachers kill as many, 'cept in a different way."

"I don't understand…"

A whiff of cigar smoke told her he still puffed on the stogie even before the red glow confirmed it.

"Figure you got as much guts as me," he said after a pause—whether to puff on the cigar or to gather his thoughts, she wasn't sure.

"Surprises me you hadn't figured this out already. That other bastard granddaughter of mine, the one living up in Little Rock, she learned about me years ago. You may be as surprised as she was to learn that I've been with you every day of your life."

Sidra tried wrapping her mind around that thought until his next words pried them loose.

"By the way, not to change the subject, but what made you marry that preacher?" He chuckled, then withdrew his hand from his jacket pocket and worried the scar down the side of his cheek.

"Does that hurt?" she asked, curious. She'd seen pictures of the scar down one side of his face and how he hated it, and hated when people called him Scarface.

"What? Does what hurt?"

"Your scar. Does—"

"Nah, habit mostly—that and touching it reminds me of the guy who did it. Never turn your back on your enemy, gal. You learned that the hard way same as me, as I recall."

"Look, Mr. Capone—"

"Get rid of the Mr. thing. I'm kin. Remember?"

"So you say. I have no idea what to call you, then. Al? Mr. Capone? Granddad?" She snickered after the last one.

"Before you so rudely interrupted, I wanted you to know I been with you all your life. Like, I seen you get run off the road down there in Texas. Helped you out that tight."

"When?"

"On that first case you took."

"That night in the ditch?" Sidra choked, on either the smoke, her own saliva, or the shock of what she'd heard. Or all three.

"Okay," she said, when she could speak again. "Tell me about her?"

"You mean your great grandmother?"

Sidra nodded.

Al's eyes took on a softened glow, his face relaxed. "She worked in the houses sometimes. Had nice curves—I never did like *stick-women*. Gimme something to hold onto."

Sidra snickered.

"Hey, don't laugh. Ever tried to hug a stick? Nothing soft about it.

"Anyway, I remember her tender smile, and the feel of the long lace dangling from the sleeves of her dress. As I said, she was older, knew how to love a man without losing herself."

He hung his head, propped his forearms on his leg. His hands dangled towards the floor. "Felt real bad I gave her the syphilis. Ended up killing her. Broke my heart, really. I always kept my ear to the ground about the baby. Knew kinfolk from Texas came got the baby. Then, course after I passed, I spent time getting to know her— and you—and your brother Warren."

"Warren? So you did know him."

Al gave a short loud belly laugh. Sidra wondered if others in the house heard him, and listened for sounds, but no one came.

"Well, I suppose the term's *know* him. Me and him talk all the time. He's quite a guy—that man. Wished I could've…well, crying over spilt milk and all that. I did work with him on a few cases—"

"Really?"

"Oh hell yeah. Helped him find that woman tied up in the barn."

The room grew quiet. Sidra wondered if she dreamed. Perhaps she did, but even if she did, what did it matter? Something about it rang true—very true.

"Tell me what it was like being a gangster." The words came unfiltered, and once out, she longed to recall them. One look at Al told her of that impossibility.

He took a big draw on his cigar, lifted his chin and allowed the smoke to swirl up and circle his head. "Bold woman, are you? What makes you think my world was any different than yours today?"

"Forgive my brash questions. My parents always told me I asked too many, some of which bordered on rude."

Al's chest puffed up and out. At first she wasn't sure if fury raged in his gut or not, and if it did, was she in danger. That is until he broke into sidesplitting laughter. "Yep, you're my kin all right. If you'd a lived during that period, I bet you'd have been a moll for sure."

"I'm sorry—"

"Don't be. Hundred years or so ago that might have got you a bullet, but I've learned a lot on the other side. Not near as touchy."

Sidra relaxed her shoulders. Somewhere in the mix, she found her breath. A sigh slipped into the room. "I don't mean to be rude, Mr.—"

"Al, Sidra. If you can't call me Gramps, Al will do just fine. Never knew how to be a grandparent anyway."

"What else do you know about my biological mother—this Miss White? I never knew anything about her. I came to Hot Springs to help my client, Belle Anderson, understand her family. I had no idea her life and mine intertwined."

Al leaned back in the rocking chair, took a big draw and exhaled again. The room grew quiet, Sidra wasn't sure if he'd heard her question.

"I'd say your past is intertwined with Miss Anderson. Her family owned these houses from the get-go. Your grandma was conceived in one of Miss Scarlet's beds."

Sidra choked. "She what…?"

"Sorry, didn't mean to shock you with that information, but truth's truth." The room grew silent. Al's thoughts looked to have traveled back in time. "Miss White was a beauty." His voice cracked with emotion. "Soft, not like the others. She held a maturity I liked. Kind heart—I guess that's what made me choose her. We'd spend hours just lying on the bed talking. She'd ask about my scar—this one on my face. Wanted to know how I got it."

"And did you tell her?"

He chuckled. "I used to tell people I got it from shrapnel when I led a charge during the war to end all wars."

"Did you?"

He shook his head and laughed. "Not even close. But I learned a big lesson from this scar."

"What?"

"Don't be a smart-ass kid, and never say something bad about a guy's sister," he bellowed. "At the time, I did it to get the boy's goat, but the only goat I got was my own. Lived with this dang reminder the rest of my life." He ran his fingers down the scar again. "People always asked why I fiddled with it. Well, it's a lesson I won't ever forget—as long as I touch it. Reminds me to mind my manners." With that, he roared with laughter.

"Am I not supposed to believe that?" Sidra leaned forward, unsure whether to join in the laughter, or keep her own mouth shut.

She changed the subject. "Why are you here?"

He snorted. "You really want to know?"

"More than anything."

"I wanted to meet you."

Sidra swallowed, hard. "Meet me?"

"Don't gotta believe me, kid, but as I said, I've been with you most all your life." He laughed. "Almost gave up and left when you married that preacher—that was taking things a bit too far—stretching your great grandpa in ways I never wanted to stretch, but…I hung in there."

He pulled his hand out of his pocket and relit the cigar. The smoke curled into his now half-lidded eyes. An intelligence, a sense of knowing—all knowing—radiated from him.

A sob escaped her lips. "I wish I'd known about you a long time ago. Maybe if we had… Sorry my family…"

"I know all about your family, doll. I was there—have been since I crossed over."

Sidra stared at him.

"Don't look dumbfounded, kid. I know, life on earth's tough. You think you got it bad—huh—what if the whole fucking world knew what a shit you were. Past and present. Yeah, I made some really stupid mistakes. Thought I was the cats meow. Crooked my finger and whatever babe I wanted came running. Except your great grandmother. Not her. I had to work for her attention."

Al scanned the room, checking, it seemed, to make sure no one was in earshot. "You get the clap—you give the clap. Sad tale, that—I killed the only woman I ever really cared about.

"Thing is, on your side, you don't see life opening up to you. You just live it, and take the steps we take, and tell ourselves we're creating our own destiny.

"I dang sure thought I was in charge of mine. My people, my gangs, my lord bosses. When you spend time on the other side, you learn life unfolds on that side, same as it does on this. We still gotta make our way into the unknown—"

He paused, took a big puff on his cigar and watched the smoke blend with the air chilling down for the night.

"You see we make our way into the unknown thinking we're some kind of big piece of shit. We think we're in charge of our lives. Ain't so. Life ain't dependent on us or anything we do. Goals—yeah, they're important, but not nearly as important as enjoyment—fully experiencing the journey we been given.

"Instead, folks like me fuck it up more and more, thinking we own the world and everybody living in it. Don't matter what they want. What matters is the bankroll in our pockets."

Sidra questioned not what the man said, but how it fit society, as she knew it. She started to say such, but before she could, his monologue continued—a monologue he appeared determined to share.

"As a kid growing up on the streets of New York, everyone seemed in a hurry—hurry to get more money, get a business going, make a name for themselves. Truth is, rushing gets you nothing but trouble." His index finger again sought the raised scar down the left side of his face. He traced it, slow and methodical, like he had memorized every jagged edge.

"Is that how you got the scar?"

He jumped, like he'd forgotten her sitting across from him, and chuckled.

"That it is, missy. That it is. Young boys get in such an all-fired hurry to get the girl—gotta take care how we do it. Saying you *mean* no disrespect, don't make it so."

"What happened?"

"I don't care to talk about the details, let's say it ain't only about the journey to get what we want, it's how we go about getting it. That's where the lessons are the strongest, even though at the time, they seem like nothing—unimportant. On the other side, I've seen how if I'd a slowed down and enjoyed every minute, instead of always pushing for more."

"Are you saying all those people you are said to have killed—"

"Now hold on there. Everybody always wants to go back to the killings. I'm done with them. I'm a different person on the other side. Learned lessons about myself. Seems I was always impatient because I couldn't control my world like I thought I should. Got rid of all those who stood in my way." He smirked. "Thing is, I didn't get rid of them at all. Still see them on the other side."

The room grew quiet as night moved into early morning. Her eyelids heavy, she allowed them to close for a moment.

"Well, time for me to leave." Al stood, tucked his hand in his coat pocket and took a couple of steps. "Wasn't supposed to even be here. *Ghosts* are for kids, you know." He stifled a chuckle. "Just thought I'd drop by and let you know you're not alone. By the way, someday you might want to ask your brother how he and I got you and Belle together."

The room grew quiet—still. Sidra sat starring at the now empty room and the ray of sunlight filtering through the old leaded glass windows.

Had he been here? If he had, what was that he said about he and Warren getting…

Had she imagined it?

Even if she had, she felt a peace about Warren's death she'd never felt. He didn't feel gone anymore. She tucked that feeling away and headed downstairs to put on a pot of coffee and see if Slider needed a potty call outside.

She rounded the small stairs to find Sawyer beat her to it. The coffee pot gurgled as he stood watch over it, cup in hand.

"Good morning, Sid. Oh, I let Slider outside. His bladder called."

When she didn't answer, Sawyer looked up at her. "Get a good night's sleep? You don't look like you did. You look like you've seen a ghost. Those women show up again?" He paused. "Even if they did, it's morning and coffee's almost ready. That'll help."

"Great! I need a cup, bad!" She laughed.

"Belle up, too? Heard your voice. Figured you would both be downstairs soon, so I put on the pot."

"You heard my voice? Only mine?" Had she been talking to herself?

"Yeah, sounded like you were talking to someone… I never heard Belle, but since she's the only other one there…"

Sidra took the proffered cup and moved to the living room. A fire already blazed. "Mmmm, fire's nice."

"You okay?" Sawyer joined her.

"Why? Do I not look like I am?" She smiled at him over the edge of her cup.

How in the world did she describe what she'd witnessed—discussed her own heritage with a ghost. No one would believe this—well, yeah, these two would.

"You heard talking upstairs okay, but did you smell cigar smoke?"

"Is that what that smell was? I wondered if someone outside was burning dry leaves this early in the morning."

"Cigar smoke. Cuban, to be exact." Would he believe her when she recounted her visitor?

"However, it wasn't Belle talking with me. It was Al Capone."

"I don't understand." Sawyer looked dumbfounded.

Sidra laughed so hard her coffee sloshed out of the

cup. "Me either!"

Belle rounded the stairs. "What's going on down here? You two sound like you're having way too much fun without me. Did I miss anything?"

"I'll say," Sawyer headed to the kitchen. "Go have a seat by the fire. I'll get you a cup of coffee. Sidra's got a lot of explaining to do."

His words sounded serious, but his smirk revealed keen interest in the upcoming topic.

"Your brother knew your lineage to Capone all along and never told you?" Belle moved to the edge of her chair when Sidra concluded the retelling of her visit with Mr. Capone. "What are the odds of you coming here to work on my case, and have a bomb dropped on you like that? Afraid I'd be furious with my brother."

Sidra gave a sardonic laugh. "I feel about the same way you felt with the bomb dropped on you by Maxx—a bomb left for him to drop, and not your parents."

"Good point, but..."

"It's uncanny, and I'm reeling," Sidra said.

Why would Warren have not told her this, especially since he knew she was coming to Hot Springs, the mobster's, her grandfather's, stomping grounds. Why did he wait and let that *dearly departed* drop the bomb?

What did all this have to do with the old woman down the hill—or was she a figment of Sidra's imagination, too?

Nothing made sense anymore. "Excuse me, folks. I need fresh air."

She grabbed her coat and scarf and went outside. Slider lay on the front porch, but when he saw her move to the steps, he joined her.

She avoided the direction of the old crone's shack—a shack that evidently didn't exist other than in her mind. Slider usually ran ahead of her, but not this time. He stayed right by her side. She walked around to the rear of the house and up the hill passed *the tree of death* where the judge executed the guilty and innocent alike, all based on his own warped sense of justice.

Justice? Was that merely a word—a long ago figment of someone's imagination carried over to modern times?

A fallen tree trunk caught her eye and she wandered over and perched on it. Slider took advantage of the opportunity and sniffed amongst the dead weeds and branches, looking back to check on her every few minutes.

The wind rustled a pile of brown leaves, scattering a handful, only to allow them to settle to earth once more, content in their life-death process and their upcoming assignment to nurture the earth. The cycle provided rich nutrients for new growth awaiting their chance in spring.

How could a man—men—her great grandfather—be responsible for mass murders, then die and come back, if not contrite, at least justify their actions? How was that different than what the judge did? Was it?

She recalled Al's words—if indeed they were words, and not figments of her weird, screwed up mind. He said he'd learned a lot since he'd left this world. Was that repentance? If so, how did that match—for lack of a better example, the smoke from his cigars? She would swear he enjoyed watching the souls of those he'd murdered—yes, Al, murdered. There's no other word to describe what you did.

"If you're not the same man you were when you walked this earth, how can you find pleasure in what you accomplished here? Tell me! Help me make sense of all this. And while you're at it, explain to me why my dear departed brother never told me about you. Why was I kept in the dark all these years—only to feel like a fool now."

Tears welled in her eyes. She swiped them with her coat sleeve.

"Dammit, I'm not going to cry. You and my brother are not going to get to me—make me feel like a fool…"

Okay, well, maybe forget that last sentence. She already felt like a fool.

Well sis, I wanted to tell you so many times—then you married that preacher. Imagine what that would have done to your reputation—not to mention his.

That image sank in a couple of seconds, until Sidra burst out laughing—so loudly Slider rushed over to check on her. He laid his nose on her thigh and looked at her, concern written all over his face.

"I'm okay, sweetheart, I just had a visual."

He took her at her word and ran off to chase a squirrel.

"Answer my question—how could Al Capone—"

What you saw was a left-behind memory of our great grandfather before he crossed over. That's not soul on the other side. Most people would have never picked up on it, but you're so damn perceptive you don't miss a thing.

"I don't understand."

That's why most of us who've crossed over don't like to come back in visual form—our past lives bump up against our spirits. It's difficult for humans in this world to sort through all that—hence the danger of being misinterpreted.

She guessed that made sense.

Our great grandfather struggled with whether or not to show up. I talked him into it because I was too chicken-shit to tell you myself.

"Were you the one who set up this whole trip? To have our great grandfather do your dirty work?"

Well, he whined, *yes and no. I nudged Belle your way because I believed you were the best one to help her— since I knew what was coming.*

"Is that supposed to be a compliment?"

Dang it, Sidra, our great grandfather asked me for a favor, okay?

"Asked you to?"

He has always regretted not being a part of your life—at least in memory. He wanted you to know about him.

"Now I know, but what do I do with that knowledge?"
You might ask him sometime.

She sat quietly after Warren finally shut up, and later turned on her cell phone. She hadn't checked her emails or messages in days and now saw numerous texts from her fiancé Ben Hillerman. He recounted the stack of mail in her office and phone calls from prospective clients. Annie was due home from her overseas jaunt any day now. When was she coming home?

One item remained—the listing of the houses.

Chapter Thirty-Six

Back at the house, Sidra found the other two packing their bags.

"What's going on?" she asked.

"Sawyer and I feel like things here are pretty much settled—at least well enough that we can head back to Texas."

"Does that mean you're ready to list these houses?"

Belle closed the trash bag and handed it to Sawyer. "I've been thinking about whether or not I want to do that."

"What did you decide?"

"I've decided they've been in my family way too many years for me to let them go. Sawyer and I have been talking about turning them into a haunted bed and breakfast. We've been looking on the internet researching the viability of that."

Sawyer, with trash bag in hand, joined in. "Seems there's a big market for them. We're going home, but only long enough to get things settled there and make plans to come back and set up the business."

"Wow." Sidra shook her head. "I sure didn't see that coming. Do you plan to run them yourself?"

"I'll hire a local manager to run it. I'm sure the realtor could help me with that. I'll come back as often as I can. I've fallen in love with the *ladies*. Add all the publicity we've received from the still unidentified remains in the basement, I think the business will boom. Hot Springs is a tourist town to start with. Hundreds of people come during horserace season. Lots of them are bound to be ghost hunters. Let them hunt here—for a nightly fee, that is."

"You do have traits of your dad in you." Sawyer laughed. "The good traits."

"And what better history than to know my good friend Sidra has ties to the town and the mob. What better publicity do I need?" She looked at Sidra. "Maybe you'll even come visit ever now then and give a history lesson, Sid."

"Maybe," Sid said, laughing. "Once I get my head around having Al Capone as a great grandfather. But do you think with all our work here, perhaps we've cleared the ghosts out?"

"Customers won't know that—and there's enough history of them that no one will care. Just have to find a good manager. Plus, if I know ghosts, they may be at rest now, but that doesn't mean this is not their home. They'll be back."

Sawyer rested the black trash bag on the floor and camped on the edge of the sofa. "What about me? Would you consider hiring me to manage them? I've kind of fallen in love with this place, and my whole perspective on life has changed. I don't want to work at the church. I want to be here—to open people's minds to life and life hereafter. There is way too much history here to just tear down these houses, I agree. If you sold them that's what an investor would do. Build a big fancy hotel atop this hill. I could give tours, presentations, and I cook a mean breakfast. I can hire someone to clean the rooms and such."

Sidra and Belle both stood with their mouths open.

"Wow, you've been giving this lots of thought." Belle plopped down beside Sawyer. "Let's do it! I'll take Sidra home, get things lined up there, and then come back."

"Hot damn!" Sawyer pounded his knee with his fist. "If you'll bring my things, and wind up the lease at my apartment, I'll stay here and get started on the website and such."

Car loaded with suitcases and dogs, Sidra and Belle headed down the hill towards Central Avenue.

"My one concern, is—you'll laugh about this, Sidra, but—the women are gone. We've cleared the ghosts. They've settled what they needed to settle. We can't sell the Painted Ladies as a haunted B&B if we've run off all the ghosts."

"You having second thoughts? You sounded so confident earlier."

"Maybe."

"It'll be okay, no one can ever guarantee a ghost will actually appear. The question of whether or not one will is a part of the mystery. It has the past stories, good and bad and the ghost tours—that will bring people in. Sometimes I think we see what we want to see. Want to see a ghost— a ghost appears. You aren't really lying—"

"Look!" Belle pointed to three familiar-looking women dressed in long, lacy outfits strolling arm in arm along the street as Sidra sped past.

She checked the rearview mirror.

Nothing.

Epilogue
Miss Fancy

Lilly, Scarlet, and I sit at my kitchen table discussing recent events—events we've long wished to occur, but now that they have, we find ourselves with mixed feelings.

"I can't decide whether to stay or go," Lilly argues. "Now that the others are gone this might not be such a bad place to live. I especially like the young woman's idea of turning us into a Haunted Bed & Breakfast." She chuckles. "Can you imagine owning a Haunted B & B and not having a single ghost show up? Phet! Big failure for sure. That might be fun to watch."

Scarlet latches onto that idea, hoots with laughter, bounces up and says, "Or it might be more fun to hang around and *haunt* the houses just for the heck of it."

"We can have fun dreaming up plenty ways to

torment tourists who come to be tormented," Scarlet adds. We don't want to disappoint them."

Horrified, I shake my head. "This is ridiculous. No. We cannot do that. It is not right."

Lilly and Scarlet laugh at me, but I don't care.

"Look, Miss Goody Two Shoes," Lilly says. "It feels dang good that we're free to cross over after being caught between worlds, our souls melding into every tiny particle of these houses."

The room grows silent, but only for a minute before Lilly continues her tirade.

"Forced to act up, slam doors, sit on the beds of visitors, cry our eyes out, reliving the horror that day Daddy got caught for killing all those men."

"What kind of daddy is that," Scarlet says, picking up the lament, "when a man shoots his three daughters, and then their mother when she goes berserk, all to save his own sorry ass."

Flames flashed behind my eyes as hot as they did that night hell came a-calling. Kerosene fumes clog my nostrils. Hordes of townsfolk marching up the hill to witness retribution, staying all night, watching Papa's house burn to the ground. Even then, the horror of his actions remained unquenched.

Of course, by then Papa'd already left town driving a team of horses as black as his heart. No matter that we were already in spirit, those flames still seared our souls and halted our passing over to the other side.

"Changing the subject," Scarlet said, interrupting my thoughts, "but what about that guy Sawyer? So he's the ancestor of our half-brother Henry. I always wished Henry hadn't run away. Poor Henry. Papa treated him worse than us. Beat him for the fun of it. Might be nice to stay behind and get to know he and Sawyer better."

Sometimes I think these sisters of mine irritate me on purpose. I slap the table with the palm of my hand. "We are not staying here, and that's final. I've had enough of this place."

"Fancy, you're not the boss of us. We can stay if we want to," Lilly argues, stubborn as all get out. "Besides, wouldn't it be fun to watch Al Capone show up and insist on helping Sidra and her brother?"

Scarlet snickered. "Yes, I'm sitting here thinking of all the fun we can have."

"Fun? Like what?" I ask.

"Like the old man in the dark coat who shows up then disappears. They haven't figured out who he is and why he comes and goes."

Lilly stomps her foot at Scarlet. "Come on, you don't know who he is either."

Scarlet's grin puts the devil to shame.

www.ingramcontent.com/pod-product-compliance
Lightning Source LLC
Chambersburg PA
CBHW070638100726
47907CB00007B/2023